Mercy Seat

For Archie,

With all my best,

Wayne.

Mercy Seat

Wayne Price

**FREIGHT
BOOKS**

First published 2015

Freight Books
49–53 Virginia Street
Glasgow, G1 1TS
www.freightbooks.co.uk

A CIP catalogue reference for this book is available from the British Library.

ISBN 978-1-908754-98-1
eISBN 978-1-908754-99-8

Typeset by Freight in Plantin
Printed and bound by Bell and Bain, Glasgow

the publisher acknowledges investment from
Creative Scotland toward the publication of this book

Wayne Price was born in south Wales but has lived and worked in Scotland since 1987. His short stories and poems have been widely published and have won many awards. His debut story collection, *Furnace*, published by Freight in 2012, was shortlisted for the Saltire Scottish First Book of the Year and longlisted for the Frank O'Connor International Short Story Award. He teaches at the University of Aberdeen. *Mercy Seat* is his first novel.

Did it wait, this mood, to mature with hindsight?
In a trance from the beginning, then as now.

Li Shang-Yin, *'The Patterned Lute'*
(ninth century)

One

I think now, nearly thirty years too late, that Christine came to us that summer not meaning to shipwreck our lives, at least not to begin with, but just to save herself somehow. Like the swimmer she was, and too far out from land, she knew she had to find something to take hold of, or drown.

For a long time I'd assumed that if there'd been any meaning at all in what happened that August, then it was something to do with control and revenge; something primitive in both Christine and me, and in Jenny too, by the end. I'm ashamed about the pettiness of those thoughts now, but maybe it's impossible to understand certain things without the years, and all their losses, to teach us. Maybe any kind of cruelty comes from simple need, and we could see it properly if we could step through its mirror, the looking-glass that only ever shows ourselves. But back then in the midst of it I was young, and dazed with responsibilities – marriage, and fatherhood – that had come too soon. I was staring out at the world as if I'd woken in a small room that wasn't my own, in a strange land, and I understood so little of what I was seeing. Maybe nothing at all.

I came to this little town by the sea as randomly as driftwood. Though I'd been bright at school, and spent most of my childhood steeped in books, I'd left at sixteen to take up an electrician's apprenticeship at the Lady

Windsor, one of the Cynon Valley collieries. It didn't take much time for me to feel that I'd escaped one prison for another, and when the long strike began a year later and I joined the pickets at the gates it felt, secretly, like a miraculous reprieve. Looking at the grim faces of the older men around me as they passed the long empty hours with gossip, politics, rugby talk and despair for the future if the strike wasn't won by Christmas, I felt almost drunk with a guilty, fugitive lightness I'd never felt before except in books and dreams, and which I sometimes think I've spent the rest of my life trying to recapture.

When the union asked for volunteers to strengthen the picket at Cynheidre Colliery in Carmarthenshire, the westernmost pit in the south Wales coalfield, I made sure to sign up. On a wet Monday morning, sometime in October, I sat with a dozen other men squeezed tight against the window of a steamy, leaking, smoke-filled minibus and imagined that all the grey spiders' nests of the valleys towns we crawled through – Porth, Ton Pentre, Treorchy – were unravelling behind us like traps of dirty silk, dissolving in the rain.

Not many weeks later I packed as much as I thought I needed to take, left a note filled with words I can't begin to remember, and rode a slow train from Cardiff to Carmarthen. I stayed a while, working and shivering through the winter on a building site, and when that job was done I carried on west until I reached the sea. I've hardly been back to the valleys since, except twice to see each of my grandparents buried, six months apart. They'd raised me since I was eleven.

That was my first betrayal I suppose, though I didn't

see it that way at the time. Part of me believed I'd be back, like a prodigal, maybe as soon as Christmas, or with the spring. It wasn't as if they'd caused me any unhappiness. In fact, for the first few years after my mother's death my grandfather was by far the most important person in my life, and they both did their best for me in their strict but kindly Baptist chapel way. Until the long, inward solitary confinement of adolescence took hold of me I even shared in my grandfather's enthusiasms. He read and passed on to me an endless stream of Westerns, dog-eared paperbacks from the local library, filled with prairie sunsets, blood-feuds and solitary Texas Rangers. Until my early teens I could lose myself utterly in them, and lived their simple dramas out in almost every daydream. The plots were as linear and satisfying as the dusty trails the white-hatted rangers followed, tracking down every kind of lawlessness to Indian camps, ghost towns, Mexican deserts, the dazzling snows of the High Sierra.

On Saturdays he took me to the matinees at the Workmen's Hall. The steep, claustrophobic little cinema, blanketed in a permanent smog of cigarette smoke, dust and the smell of mothballs, was set up on those mornings purely for an audience of retired or invalided miners. Ancient Mrs Protheroe, who'd lived just a few doors up from my mother and me when I was small, tottered about as the usher and made sure no teenagers slipped in to make use of the darkness at the back. Monday nights it was all theirs, but the Saturday matinees were sacrosanct and the place was a fuggy temple of hacking coughs, old men's muttered greetings, and 1940s Americana – a double bill of Roy Rogers and Clayton Moore as The Lone Ranger if we were lucky, or The Three Stooges, or Abbott and

Costello. I remember we both despised any love interest, any sentimental complication. My grandfather would let out a soft, but quite audible angina moan that always sounded strangely private to me, as if it came from behind the door of a locked toilet cubicle. He would shift a little in his seat and I would stare at my knees and fill my head with other, manly thoughts until the embarrassment was over. Actually, not just embarrassment. It was a kind of physical dread. It gripped my throat and sometimes made me want to run from the cinema, though it pinned me helpless in my seat. A slow kiss or confession of love on that big, glowing screen would disturb me more than any kind of cliff-hanger or violence, and I could never bear to witness it.

One summer holiday I devoted several days to memorising the Lone Ranger's Moral Code, then greatly pleased my grandfather by being able to recite it to him like a catechism. Most of it has crumbled from my mind now, but I still recall the first of them: *To have a friend, a man must be one.* And the precept that puzzled me most and haunted me as a boy: *Sooner or later... somewhere... somehow... we must settle with the world and make payment for what we have taken.*

He introduced me to music, too – my grandfather I mean, though his and the Lone Ranger's tastes might well have coincided. His great favourites were Hank Williams and Jimmie Rodgers – tough, doomed country kids who would have been the same ripe old age as him if they hadn't burned themselves through and died young, decades before that kind of waste became so fashionable in my own world. Their scrubbed, narrow faces stared out from the well-thumbed album covers at me as my grandfather read, for the thousandth time, the liner notes on the backs. I could probably still sing along to 'Ramblin' Man', 'Prairie Lullaby', and 'I'm So Lonesome I Could Die'.

As I grew into my teens I began avoiding our Saturday rituals (the same way, a few years earlier, I'd begun to find excuses for missing chapel services on Sundays and Prayer Meeting on Thursdays), preferring to hide away in my back bedroom with a record player, and records, of my own. It wounded him a little to begin with, I think, but he was wise enough not to fight it or mock my new obsessions. They were already twenty years out of date, but seemed dizzyingly prescient to me: Dylan, of course, Joni Mitchell, Hendrix, Cohen and Neil Young; and then, following their clues, the second-hand Sun Records I scrabbled for like a prospector at the backs of musty enthusiast shops. As soon as I began earning a little money of my own from paper rounds I'd catch a bus and a train to Cardiff one Saturday a month and walk a circuit of them all, those secretive little import and bootleg record stores that seem to have almost vanished from the earth now. I'd trudge miles between them, in sunshine or rain, from the back streets of Canton and Cathays to the winding city centre arcades. And then finding the old Blues men in those same plywood racks: Blind Willie Johnson growling 'John the Revelator', Memphis Slim, Champion Jack Dupree. For years in my teens those voices, crackling like messages from another planet through my boxy Philips stereo, were all I wanted in the endless evenings for company.

When I left my grandparents' house I left music behind, too. I had no practical way of taking it with me, for one thing, but more than that I lost any sense of need for it, and that feeling has stayed with me ever since. I stopped looking for myself in songs the same way I stopped looking for myself in the Lone Ranger's code, or my grandmother's bible stories. Even a jukebox in a bar, if it plays a song I remember, can make me feel suddenly sick with impatience, anxious to be gone, like being persuaded too insistently about something you already, long ago and irrevocably, had decided.

*

It was a local man – one of the younger farmers I sometimes fell in with at the beach front bars, down from the fields on a one-night tear – who told me about Pugh's farm at Fynnon-wen, high up in the Rheidol hills. One of the two middle-aged sons had hanged himself in the barn, just a month before, he said. There was work on the place for sure, he reckoned, if I could get along with that mad old bugger Pugh – a long-time widower – which he doubted. He laughed as he said it, but I wrote down the directions, and his name as a kind of reference.

The next day, a Sunday, I waited at the gate of old man Pugh's yard at noon, ankle-deep in mud, until the frantic barking of his dogs drew him out of one of the low, rusting sheds. Tall, completely bald and stooping in the fine, blowing drizzle amongst his yapping border collies looked as if he'd stepped straight out of the nineteenth century: above his high, caked boots he wore a narrow black suit, shiny with God knows how many years of use, and a grey, collarless shirt that must once have been black too, buttoned tight at the neck. His white face was long and horse-like, sprouting even whiter, sparse whiskers about the chin, and his pale, watering eyes looked as if they'd been soaked and stained in some antique wooden wash-tub with his shirt. I wondered if he was still dressed in mourning for his son, or if this was his Sunday outfit, but in fact through all the time I knew him, occasional changes of shirt or the addition of a black, tent-like rain cape aside, I never saw him dressed differently.

He stared towards some far-off point behind me, somewhere in the steep green woods across the deep cut of the valley, as I gabbled about needing a few months of work, and my competence at labouring, basic handiwork, electrics and so on. I'd given it up as a wasted journey by the time I'd run out of things to say, but when I finally mentioned that all I needed was enough money to feed myself through the week and a place to sleep, his eyes locked back into focus and he shifted his colourless stare full on to my face.

Twenty pounds, he said, then shifted the wet gravel in his throat and spat. Twenty pounds a week.

I didn't reply. I hadn't hoped for much, but even in those days the amount was barely enough to live on.

And breakfast, see. He made a slow, sideways chewing motion with his long chin. And supper, maybe, he added doubtfully, if you make it for all of us, and it's not some kind of muck you serve up. Cawl, we like.

I nodded, though I knew only the basics of frying and boiling. Where would I stay? I asked.

He grunted and jerked his head back towards the shed he'd emerged from, then turned without opening the gate and stumped toward it.

I unbolted the heavy steel bars and followed, the dogs swirling around my legs and almost tripping me into the filth. To my great relief he carried on past the ramshackle hut and led me through a screen of hazels to a narrow, sheltered patch of grass where a bulbous little caravan sat, once white but greening over now with a thin skin of mould.

Old Pugh halted before it and waited for me to catch up.

I stopped at his shoulder and we both gazed at the fat tin mushroom as if it had just fallen from the moon. God knows how he'd managed to set it there: I could see no clear path through the stunted trees all around. It might have sprouted up in the rain that cool wet morning. The dogs had vanished along the way. I hadn't noticed them going, but it was very quiet now, the rain too soft to make a sound on the roof of the caravan.

It's not locked, he said.

And so I worked as a farm-hand, or a shepherd as I liked to think of it, through the spring and early summer of 1985, in a place hardly touched by three quarters of a century, rounding up stray ewes on the bald hills, or coppicing the tangled blackthorns and hazels with a rusty blade from the barn, or sweating over another bubbling pot of mutton or rabbit cawl in the gloomy, brooding evenings. Sometimes the remaining son, Meirion – a slow, silent hulk of a man – would be set to work alongside me on the heavier jobs, but most days old Pugh kept us apart. I was glad: once, hammered awake out of the caravan's damp bed in the early hours to help with spring lambing in the barn, I watched Meirion kneel beside a panting, glassy-eyed ewe that was struggling to give birth, force his huge thumb a little way inside the bulging vent and break the newborn's trapped neck with a single sharp press. *Marw-anedig*, he grunted to the old man who was busy with another birth, and leered up at me when he heard his father groan and curse. I knew he'd have been more than happy to do the same to my own spine, and turned away, saying nothing. I suppose he wanted the farm to fail – or at least wanted the old man to give up at last and sell, freeing him into some other imagined life. Or it was an impulse, and there was no more sense in it than in the way he would wander the boundary hedges some evenings, thrashing at the birds' nests in them with a heavy sickle.

It was late June of that year, a warm day of tall blue skies, when I first met Jenny. It must have been a Sunday because I had the whole afternoon and evening to myself – Sunday was the one night in the week I didn't need to brew up more cawl because of the heavier midday meal – and as usual on any day off that was fine I'd walked the mile or so downhill to Devil's Bridge where I could catch the bus or hitch a ride into town. From the promenade I'd climbed Constitution Hill and meant to follow the cliff-top path to Clarach Bay, but the sound of talk and laughter lured me down like a siren song from the main path to a small rocky cove. Six or seven young men and women – students I supposed, finished with their exams – were sunbathing and swimming from a long dark platform of stone. I remember being surprised at myself, embarrassed in fact, for needing company, or even just the spectacle of it, so badly. But the truth is I was growing strange in the pale little capsule of Pugh's caravan: often when I found myself needing to interact in the simplest ways with people outside the world of the farm or the solitude of the hills – buying a bus ticket, say, or the rare luxury of a newspaper – I'd be suddenly tongue-tied, overcome with a sense of trying to communicate through a wall of glass, or fathoms of water.

I must have sat watching them, drinking up the sound of their laughter and banter, for a good half hour. They noticed me, but paid no attention. I'd closed my eyes and was drifting into a half-sleep when Jenny, maternal even then, touched me on the shoulder and laughed when I startled. She was holding a half-full bottle of wine, and pushed it towards me as my eyes adjusted to the dazzle.

Are you finished too? she said.

Oh. No, I managed to answer. No, I'm not a student.

She eyed me more closely, grinning, and gestured with the bottle again, though all I could think about was the light cotton skirt fluttering against her legs, almost transparent in the sun, and the cups of her pink bikini top above it, filled with the heavy cream of her breasts. I'd never been with any girl or woman, and though I can smile at my ogling now, on that sunstruck afternoon her bare skin amazed me like a vision. Go on – have a drink, she insisted and then, when I finally took the wine from her, eased herself down to sit next to me. She spoke with a warm, thick valleys lilt, and I was amazed at the wave of homesickness – all its choking brine – that the sound of her voice sent crashing through me. I sat and listened like a child.

Though she was curious to see it, I never let Jenny visit the caravan. The thought of Meirion prowling outside with his sickle was one good reason, and my toilet situation was the other, since all I had was a tin pail under the dripping hazels – bracing but unromantic. Instead, we met in town every Sunday after that, rain or shine. She lived in a student bedsit guarded by a skinny, walking corpse of a landlady who rented out most of the rooms in her narrow three-story townhouse near the station. Mrs Horace was her name, The Horror to her tenants, mainly because she felt duty-bound to lurk outside their doors, clearing her throat noisily, if she knew one of her girls had a male visitor. But Jenny rented a basement room and her front window was a simple hop down from the pavement; it opened just wide enough for me to squirm in across a desk and onto the floor, so most often we were left in peace. Until Jenny's graduation later that summer I think we were blindly happy with each week's stolen few hours – the urgent, furtive romance of it all. Jenny being the first girl I ever properly knew, or thought I knew, I had nothing to compare it to, anyway.

In the weeks after her graduation – an English degree – Jenny toyed with the idea of moving back to Merthyr where her mother taught at the local primary school, and maybe getting work as a classroom assistant while she figured out her options for the future. But soon after, the first chill of autumn began to blow in for blustery wet days on end and Jenny took it into her head that it would kill me to stay out at the farm into winter. I laughed at her predictions of the caravan blowing down the mountain with me like a rattle inside it, or of my freezing to death in the first cold snap, but underneath my joking I was a little frightened too; not so much of the weather, but of the long dark nights to come with only the old man and Meirion for human company, each orbiting the flimsy caravan, field to stony field, in their own private, deeper winters. One Sunday at the end of September, Jenny told me she'd decided to take a secretarial job with the local council, and wanted us to look for a place together, maybe a bedsit big enough for two, and then a flat, later, if I could find work in town that paid well enough. She was already pregnant in fact, but hadn't told me. Out of pride I told her I'd think about it through the week, but really there was no choice to make.

The day I left, old Pugh said nothing as he handed over my twenty pound note, but his long chin moved with that way he had of chewing on air, or on whatever words he kept locked in his mouth. After a moment's hesitation he took a small folding knife from his pocket – a stubby, heavy, old-fashioned thing with a worn bone handle and a thick blade curved like a hawk's beak. It was the kind of hook you might use to dig a sharp stone from a hoof, and he handed it to me in a clumsy, thrusting movement. I was astonished, but took it from him with a mumbled *diolch*. I kept it with me for years, until it was stolen along with my backpack while I slept in some barn in the Basque hills; long enough I'm sure to have outlived the old man.

*

Within a week I'd found work – part-time but steady – at a warehouse on the edge of town. It was owned by Mr Anzani, who ran a cafe and delicatessen on the High Street but made his real money from wholesale supply: before the big chains like Costco and Makro took over and squeezed him back into retail, he was the hub for just about every coffee shop and deli on the Ceredigion coast, and inland to Lampeter. He'd come to Wales from Sicily as a child, and was fond of telling me how his first job had been as a delivery boy for his uncle, an ex-prisoner of war who'd stayed on after his release and opened an ice-cream shop in Mountain Ash, just six or seven miles from where I was born. That tickled him. I didn't tell him my father must have bought ice-cream there when he was a boy because he'd been brought up in a nearby street, but the thought of it unsettled me and Anzani's reminiscences always left me restless for hours after I escaped them.

My first day there a little old woman, stooped and frail, but dressed very smartly in dark maroon, came in off the street and abused me in Italian before shuffling back out again. By my second week in the job she was turning up quite regularly, and was getting more confident, haranguing me in English too. By then I'd found out from one of the van drivers that she was Anzani's ancient, crazy mother and her fussing was because the business had been milked in some small way by the warehouseman I'd replaced. So I paid no attention. At least it broke the monotony of the work a little. If I was high up amongst the crates taking inventory she'd get particularly infuriated, and would break into shrill, stilted English. Hey! You! Why you sitting up there like a mohnkey?

I'm counting the crates, Mrs Anzani. I need to see behind the crates.

What? What are you saying? Why don't you get down? Get down you lazy mohnkey!

We went through the same routine at least once a week, and in the end I'd get tired and climb down and shift a few boxes to the loading bay to calm her down.

I lied to Jenny about the hours I worked: my first lie to her, and harmless enough, I thought. I liked to be able to wander off and have time alone after my shifts, time where nobody knew or cared what I might be doing or where I might be found. It was a token freedom, I suppose. The warehouse stood at the foot of a hill, next to the clatter of a tyre-fitter's and near the furthest point of a straggling, scrubby golf course that had its club-house above the harbour, half a mile away. There was rarely anyone around except for the slow moving mechanics and maybe the odd rambler cutting in from the coast across the golf links and ambling back into town. After finishing my shift I'd often make my way up the grassy slope to the ninth hole with its tattered red flag and then climb a little way beyond it, easing sideways between bushes of gorse and broom, to a small clearing, a sun-trap in the late afternoons, where I could sit and daydream, or brood. Sometimes I'd steal a bottle or two of Peroni and a jar of olives to take with me. Until the first hard frosts set in, the gorse around the clearing was often busy with big, black heather gnats: clumsy fliers, trailing their long, broken-looking legs behind them, bumping from one late yellow flower to another. I liked to watch them stumbling amongst the thorns; they seemed drunk and peaceful from the sweet coconut smell of the blossoms.

We were in Jenny's single bed when she told me she was pregnant. By then she was two months gone and already through the morning sickness, which I'd noticed but had been too ignorant to understand. You were still working on the farm when it must have happened, she said. It was the day we walked to Clarach and it rained, and the cows followed us through the field when we took a shortcut on the way back. Remember how frightened I was? I thought we'd slip in the mud and they'd trample us.

I didn't answer and we lay there silent a while in the dark. It was a warm night for late autumn and neither of us could sleep. After a time she said, I'm keeping it, anyway, whatever happens.

I turned onto my back and stared up at the low ceiling. It occurred to me that I'd never noticed anything specific about the room before. It was simply the place where I came to lose myself in Jenny, and all its physical features had always been a blur of vague impressions: its stuffy warmth, its lingering, faint smells of perfume, nail varnish and sandalwood joss sticks, the wobbling desk in front of the window that every Sunday I wriggled my stomach across and over; the dip in the middle of the bed where the springs had failed, probably years before we ever had the use of it. And the light shade, I noticed now: colourless in the near dark, but pale and fringed with short, braided cords, some of them tangled. It looked oddly familiar and I wondered if my grandparents had a similar light shade in their own bedroom. I wondered what colour it became in the day.

What are you thinking? she said.

Nothing bad.

Then tell me.

Well, I'm thinking I don't mind. I'll help you, I said.

You don't mind, she breathed into my shoulder. I could feel the words on my bare skin.

You know what I mean, I said. I mean I'm happy about it.

Is that what you meant?

Yes. That's what I meant.

I wanted to rub my shoulder where her breathing was tickling it. I lifted my other arm across my chest and put the back of my hand between my shoulder and her breath, and I remember her kissing the knuckles in the silence, very lightly, each in turn.

Two

I wake sweating from a dream of drowning under waves.

I close my mouth and wait for my heart to settle. The room's already warm and half-lit by the early sun. I glance sideways at the clock. It's just before five. Jenny lies like a dead thing on my right and I turn my head to look at her. It seems a long time since I saw her so deep in sleep.

I try to relax myself – knotted shoulders, arms and legs – then peel the sheet from my wet skin and roll carefully out of bed. I pad across the thin carpet to the window. The yellow curtains make the light inside seem late and warm, but when I shift them there's a dead white sky. Down below the tide is right up, glutting in and out of the big grey boulders along the prom. The boulders look new and fresh-cut. They've been there a few years now but nothing sticks to them, no seaweed or limpets, except maybe on the undersides where it stays cool and damp. They stretch out in a long, clean curve all the way up to the sands and the pier. I stand there for a while against the windowsill and watch the water slip in and out between them, slow and smooth like oil. The prom and the road are still littered with debris from the storm three nights before, scraps of dried out seaweed and long snakes of gravel. The last day Christine woke in this room, and stood at this window, I can't help thinking, and feel the familiar twist in my stomach. It's calm outside now – not even a ripple on the sea – and any sounds from the water down below are too soft to carry up to the window. The sweat prickles as it dries on my bare back and a sudden, deep shiver works out from my shoulder blades and along my arms. I press my palms against the sill as if I could earth the tremor through the wood. After a while Jenny mumbles something, but when I turn she's still sleeping blind and I cross the room quietly to the door.

Outside, the landing and stairs are much darker than the room and there's a stale biscuity scent coming up off the carpet. It's a smell that builds every night but vanishes during the day. In the stillness I can hear the hot water pipes sounding through the depths of the building: a faint rattle way down on the ground floor, rising to a solid knocking behind the wall across the stairwell. It's a tall, narrow guest house – a slice of what must have been a fairly grand hotel when it was still joined to the guest houses either side – thrown up in a rush for Victorian trippers when the town was briefly fashionable, and getting cranky in its old age now. Almost any time I see Mr Clement, the landlord, he's carrying his handyman's bag of tools, off to crouch stiffly in front of another leaking cast-iron radiator, or blocked waste pipe – a long, losing battle. The bathroom is up another short flight of stairs. I slip along the passage, past the half-open door of Alex, the young student teacher, then onto the stairs and up.

In the bathroom I lift the gluey toilet seat with the back of my thumbnail, noticing the bath tub at my side is still full of greyish, used water from the night before. When I finish I drain the bath as well as flushing the toilet. I find myself watching the water level drop with absolute attention, as if there were secrets at the grimy bottom of it. The small window above the sink is jammed open and in the yard below, five floors down, Clement's Alsatian starts barking, snapping me out of my trance. Maybe it's heard the water emptying through the pipes. I decide not to go back to bed. I think of Jenny's warm body turning to me, stale with sleep, and it feels a relief to be naked and cold instead, hearing the dog – alert, and with no thought at all in its animal head – barking out its place in the world far down in the yard.

Back in the bedroom I manage to dress without waking Jenny, then go through to the sitting room. Michael lies sprawled belly-up in the cot, his wide head tilted back, eyelids sunk. I know he'll wake crying. It seems strange to see the cot back in here now Christine has gone. I cover Michael with a knitted blanket he's kicked halfway through the little wooden bars. He doesn't stir, and I'm grateful. I look over at the sofa. In the gloom I half expect Christine's shape to be still curled under sheets just a step away. Then I concentrate on what I'm doing, which is covering Michael with a second blanket, stupidly, because he'll be too hot and wake, but I do it anyway before going through to the box-room to study.

When we moved here, Jenny persuaded me to start a few courses with the Open University. You can't keep working in that warehouse all your life, she said, reasonably enough, and it was true I was getting bored, slowly but surely, with a life that was purely physical, other than when I escaped into the novels she'd kept from her student days.

As soon as I began studying again I understood that what I'd hated about school wasn't the learning after all, but just the awful sociability of school life – the constant, sparrow-like jostling and pecking that left me numb at the end of every weekday afternoon. Maybe if I'd been brought up in a younger household it would have been different; but the contrast between my grandparents' lives – they were old even for grandparents – and the lives of everyone else around me seemed to coat my schooldays in a thin wash of unreality. It was chronic loneliness I suppose, or rather chronic aloneness – I didn't think of myself as lonely because the last thing I wanted was company. There must have been others around me who felt the same way, but I never met them, or never recognized meeting them.

I chose options in History for my university courses, just because it was the subject that had held my attention best at school. It didn't matter to Jenny that I wasn't studying anything vocational, something that might spring me out of Anzani's warehouse: I think she believed that study was an end in itself and one day soon, somehow, it would begin to change my life.

If I wasn't at the warehouse or looking after Michael, the study packs that arrived every few weeks in the post took up my full attention, almost to the point of obsession, though now I remember almost nothing of what I learned. It belonged purely to that time, maybe, and once it was over, all that knowledge, all those facts and stories, dissolved into a kind of ghostliness along with everything else.

At half past six I stop what I'm doing, which isn't much apart from staring into space and thinking, and decide to go and buy milk from the nearby newsagent's on the corner. I know it'll be open by now – the paper boys trailing in to collect their heavy sacks before school. I like slipping out this early, unnoticed. It reminds me of my time on Pugh's farm, that other world, when the days started with the light and ended with the dark. It feels like a life I read about, and imagined as vividly as a child, rather than lived in the flesh.

On the way downstairs the rest of the guesthouse is still quiet, but when I get to the ground floor I hear Clement's daughter, a heavy, dour woman in her twenties, saying something behind the closed door of their shared flat. Then her own child, a plump blond toddler I sometimes catch sight of in the hall, answers back with a petulant yell. I take the front door off the latch and open it carefully, not wanting to be heard. The air's still and heavy-feeling, and I wonder if more storms are on the way.

Down on the pavement there are still a few fragments of starfish littered around, left over from the last blow-up. They get washed over the wall sometimes this time of year, hundreds of them, then dry out on the prom where kids use them like frisbees, though they only last one throw. I cross the road and head up towards the town, every now and again glancing down over the sea wall. For a while a small flatfish cruises along the same way, following the line of the stones, then one of the sunken boulders blocks it and it turns lazily back out to sea.

When I get back with the rolls Jenny's still sleeping, and suddenly I wonder if she's taken anything. She used to like to knock herself out when things got bad, but stopped after she knew she was pregnant. I decide to let her sleep till the alarm, then if that doesn't work, take another look. Michael looks very still too, though while I was out he's turned to lie flat on his stomach, head twisted to one side. I put the milk in the mini fridge then close myself in the box-room and stare at the latest of my study packs. Something about Russia, my topic for that term: these days, if I ever read anything about the czars, the Moscow winters or the big, empty steppe, I'm always reminded incongruously of that summer, and the wife and child I had so briefly, and the small, musty rooms we lived in looking out over the sea.

Michael wakes and cries just before eight. I finish the paragraph I'm reading and get up, but just as I move from the small desk I hear Jenny walking through from the bedroom to lift him up. I stay where I am and listen to her comforting him. Luke? she says, in a voice that seems to come from miles away. Luke? Are you in there? It's already a familiar tone now, that flat, far-off note in the way she calls my name, though I couldn't have said that before Christine arrived, hardly more than a week ago. I wait a moment then say, I'm here, and open the door.

While we eat breakfast Jenny tells me about her dream – Christine climbing through the window, though we're sixty feet up, getting into bed and crouching on her chest. Then Chris was a cat, Jenny says, and she was so heavy I couldn't breathe.

I nod, force myself to spoon in a mouthful of cereal.

She was this cat called Max we used to have when we were girls.

She pauses to wipe a slick of dribble from Michael's chin. The cat was on my chest but over at the wash-basin in the corner of the room at the same time, she says, watching my face as she speaks. It was sucking at the tap, which made me panic for some reason, and in the dream I was crying because Max had turned against me. I was upset about Max, not Christine, she says, as if that's the key point she wants me to understand.

She concentrates on working some softened rusk into

Michael's mouth. I notice how her own mouth opens in sympathy with his.

I don't say anything. I don't want to eat, but I chew another spoonful down.

I haven't thought about Max for years and years, Jenny goes on. He was never even there, around the house. She scoops a drool of paste from Michael's bottom lip, then feeds it back to him. Max was a real tomcat. He was never about. She scrapes around the Tupperware bowl with the spoon. He was a big ginger tom, she says.

She doesn't mention Christine apart from her being in the dream, before she became Max, but not Max, and we finish breakfast in silence. That's where the last two weeks belong now, she wants me to understand; in a bad dream that doesn't make any sense, in a story that she can end.

By the time she leaves for work Michael's calm again and I can read while he dozes in his cot. My mind won't settle though and all I find myself doing for the next hour or so is making endless rounds of the living room, like a fish in a bowl, stopping each time at Michael's cot to check on him.

Finally, as if he can sense me looming there, Michael's eyelids snap open. He fixes me for a second with an alert, adult stare, then bawls.

For once I'm glad of the chance to pick him up and hush him. I take him with me around the room a few times and when he's quietened down I take him to the window and try to interest him in the gulls and pigeons down below us on the seafront.

The inside sill is just wide enough for him to be rested on. The sun's much stronger now and I have to squint to bear the dazzle off the sea. The tide's already well out.

It must have been on the turn when I saw it lapping the wall just after dawn. The hours seem to have accumulated rather than passed, building up like a gradual, physical weight in my blood and brain, and I feel a deep sinking tiredness spread through me. Far out in the bay there's a small motorboat heading south along the coast. It's too early for paddlers or swimmers yet, and it's a weekday morning anyway, but a few early sunbathers are lying half-dressed on the sand and shingle between the boulders and the sea-line.

I look down at Michael. He's reaching for a crisp dead fly lying belly-up at the corner of the sill. It's well out of his reach so I don't need to bother with it. I yawn, then yawn again, helplessly. The boat's almost disappeared now, into the haze around the headland.

Though he can't have the fly, Michael seems peaceful enough. I take a last look out of the window, down at the pensioners, dog walkers and mothers with baby-buggies all wandering the prom. Then I take Michael over to the sofa with me, to Christine's bed when she was here, just a bare few days ago, and lay my face on the cushion – her pillow for the nights she stayed – and half believe the dusty scent I'm inhaling is part of her. I hold Michael against my chest and we sleep facing the blue sky beyond the window.

Late in the morning the shared phone in the corridor wakes me, my heart racing, and I realise that even in my sleep I was alert and listening for this, for Christine. Somehow, I stop myself going to it. Having Michael beside me, still sleeping, helps. I know there's no one else on the floor at this time of the day and soon it'll have to stop. Michael's face is turned to mine. In his open mouth I can see the smooth doll's teeth and where they haven't come yet I see the pink, smoothly swollen gums. The ringing makes me feel nauseous and for an instant I imagine Michael's milk-teeth mashing the fly on the sill. I close my eyes and wait, watching little scars of light float across the insides of my lids. I try to concentrate on them, on their jumps and drifts, and finally the ringing stops and I touch my face to the back of Michael's head.

In primary school I shared a desk for a while with a new boy: an English lad called Simon. His family came to the village – God knows why – from Hemel Hempstead, which by itself would have been enough to set him apart, but he was a misfit anyway. His high, piping voice, his plump little body and effeminate manners made him the target for all kinds of bullying, and sometimes he had fits where he'd foam at the mouth in the middle of the playground. But what was most interesting to me was being able to inspect the small, round white scars peppered on the skin behind his ears. They were smooth and a little hard to the touch. He used to boast that his father put them there with a lit cigarette when he was a baby, to get rid of his warts, he explained in all innocence, and I think it must have been true because they were about the right size. I saw his father often enough because he seemed to spend most days walking the family dog – a straining little terrier called Prince – up and down the long street we both lived on, and Simon's story interested rather than shocked or frightened me. If I was with Simon – maybe walking home from school together – and we passed his father, the two of them would acknowledge each other with a quick, discreet nod, nothing more, which I found deeply impressive. There was a kind of dignified, adult mystery about the gesture, and for a while I remember imitating the nod whenever the three of us crossed paths. I used to imagine that his father would notice me by the signal and understand I was in on their pact, whatever that was.

In the last few days she was here, Christine did things to Michael. Not like Simon's father: she didn't mark him, and Jenny never saw anything she told me about, but she sensed it. It was the reason Christine left when she did. I came in from the warehouse one afternoon to find Jenny yelling at her, not accusing her of anything directly; just telling her to leave him well alone. She stopped when she noticed I'd let myself in, and I pretended not to understand what was going on. Christine was sitting very upright on the sofa, dull-eyed and pale.

I try to push the memory down. I'm sweating now, and Michael feels like a stone on my chest. I move my face away from Michael's warm, rusk-scented head and study it. Under the wispy fair hair around the temple his pale blue veins are visible, branching under the white skin like patterns on an eggshell.

Suddenly the phone clamours into life again, jangling like an alarm, and this time Michael wakes and grizzles and pushes feebly at my locked arms. As if that breaks a kind of spell I roll us both forward and lower him crying to the carpet. Then I make for the phone, unsteady after lying still for so long.

I feel my throat almost paralysed with panic as I pick up the receiver, but it's only Jenny on the other end.

You're there, she says. I was just about to give up.

I lean a hand against the wall to steady myself. The thick patterns on the Anaglypta wallpaper feel reassuring.

I was through in the box room, I lie.

How's Michael?

He's fine. He's sleeping.

Good.

I wonder if I should ask if it was her that phoned earlier. I decide that if she did, she'll mention it, so I keep quiet. Is anything wrong? I say.

No – I had five minutes and just thought I'd ring. I was thinking about you both.

In the background somebody in the office calls something to her, but the words are too muffled to make out. Her own voice becomes distant for a moment as she turns away from the mouthpiece and asks, what was that? to whoever spoke. She laughs abruptly, her voice still angled away from the phone. Then she's back. Sorry, she says. Listen, I was wondering if you wanted to meet for lunch. It's such a nice morning, I was thinking you could bring Michael and we could sit outside with a drink maybe.

I don't answer straight away – we never meet at lunch times any more, especially now that Michael has to be brought along, and I wonder what's going on in her mind. What's made you think of that? I say, more abruptly than I mean to and immediately regretting it.

Well, don't if you don't want. Her sigh crackles down the line. It's a nice day, and I don't think it'll last, that's all.

I don't mean I don't want to. I was just surprised.

Well, but if it's awkward.

It's not awkward, I say. It's a good idea. Where do you want to meet?

I don't know. Maybe The Half Moon? In the beer garden. At one.

Right. I'll get ready.

Thanks, she says.

I picture the other workers in her office listening in to her thanking me, and wondering at it. For a difficult second or two I don't know what else to say. I'd better go and sort Michael out, I manage at last. Bye, I say, and put the receiver down.

Back in the living room Michael's found his way to the fridge. I go over to him and scoop him away. I check him to see if he needs changing, but he's clean so I lay him on his back in the cot. I feel almost frantic and can't understand why, but I know it's something to do with having expected to hear Christine's voice, not Jenny's, and having almost prepared myself to deal with that.

As soon as Michael realises I'm putting him back in the cot he starts bawling again, and when I set him down his face colours up red as a welt and he starts thrashing around as wild as all the turmoil in my head.

Christ, Michael, I say, and lift him out again. I can feel my heart working like an engine in my chest. I walk around with him for a while, letting him calm down. It's okay, I say to him. It's okay, okay, okay. You're coming too.

In the middle of the room I glance up from his shoulder and catch sight of my face in the mirror. I look furtive: narrow-eyed, like some animal slinking off with its prey. I turn Michael round to our reflections. Look, Michael, I say, trying to force some cheer into my voice. Who's that then? Who's that looking at us? Who's that?

Three

I was in bed when Christine first arrived. I'd started going down with a virus about a week earlier – chicken pox probably, though I never got it diagnosed – and that morning it had broken out in small pink body-sores.

Jenny led the way in, carrying the case, and Christine followed, smiling, alert. She peered intently at everything around her – the patterns on the lurid 1970s carpet, the big old Bakelite light switches, bulbous and stiff as breasts on a ship's figurehead, the rickety sideboard, even the regulation steel bracket that pulled the door shut behind them with a sigh and a thump. She stared as if it was all completely exotic to her, and all the functions of things were obscure. It made me wonder if she'd ever seen the inside of a hotel before. It was nearly noon but the room was curtained and gloomy and must have smelled of both Michael and me having lain there all day. I think I was the last thing she gave her specimen-collector's attention to.

Here she is, the long lost little sister, Jenny announced. She dropped the case and hugged Christine, as if performing for me, then stepped back to admire her. She was nervous and breathless, but happy.

Christine's smile didn't change. She had a mousy, innocent face, and the smile just about revealed the white glint of her front teeth.

I told her you were on your deathbed, Jenny went on.

Sorry, I said to Christine. Nice to meet you anyway.

Open the curtains maybe.

Christine looked at Jenny, and Jenny went over to let some light in. Then she opened the window wide. It's such a lovely day, she said and turned to her sister. You've been lucky, she told her. It would be nice if it lasts all the time you're here, but I doubt it. It changes all the time, doesn't it? She turned to me for confirmation.

I agreed and Christine shrugged slightly. It wouldn't matter, she said.

And here's my lovely Michael, Jenny announced with a sort of flourish, as if to show she'd saved the best for last. She moved to the bed where he'd been sleeping beside me and lifted him, just waking now with a quiet grumble, up to her shoulder.

Christine's expression didn't change at all. The same shy grin. She took a step forward and stared dutifully at the back of Michael's head.

Jenny rocked him gently, sniffed him, then offered him to her sister. His nappy's clean, she said. You're a *good* boy, she told Michael as she let go.

Right from the start, I remember, there was a kind of awkward reserve about the way Christine handled him, as if she was too conscious of indulging a desire. She wouldn't lose herself, wouldn't give anything of herself away even to a sleepy baby. Michael, I think, loved it – loved the relief maybe from the needier love of his mother. And Jenny sensed it too. I remember her look of mild surprise as Michael stopped squirming in Christine's slim arms, then the wavering, pained smile appearing on her lips as her baby lay pinned and biddable under her sister's cool, teasing stare.

You're good with him, Jenny said at last. He likes you.

You're lucky – mostly he gripes if he's away from me. He even makes a fuss with Luke sometimes. Doesn't he? she said to me.

I agreed.

Christine laughed lightly.

I'll just get up, I said.

Jenny took Michael back, jiggled him, then settled him on the bed. He was kicking but not yelling. She laid him down and he quieted.

Let's see your back, she said to me. She seated herself behind me on the edge of the bed.

I sat up straight and shifted forward, letting her run her fingers over the sores. Most of them were in a band around my waist and the small of my back.

They're like chicken pox, aren't they? she said. There was a murmur of agreement and I realised Christine had moved behind me too, leaning inwards across the bed.

Don't move, Jenny said, and I felt breath on my shoulder. Whose? I wondered. They've not got any bigger, she went on. Are they itchy?

No. Not really.

She ran a fingertip over a cluster of them. You've gone skinny again, she said.

I nodded.

Do you feel like eating? Christine didn't have anything on the train, so I'll go and buy something nice soon.

Don't you go, said Christine. I'll go and get something for us.

There's no need. Stay and talk to Luke. I can go, or there's plenty of boring food in the cupboards.

I'd like to go, she said, and this time Jenny let it pass.

They're dry, anyway, she said, touching the sores again.

I never had chicken pox, so I don't know if that's what it is. You never did either, did you? she said to Christine.

No, Christine murmured.

I don't think you ever had anything. You were never ill, were you?

Christine laughed. I must have been sometimes. I don't know.

No, Jenny said, more definite this time. I don't remember you ever being ill.

I don't know.

There was a brief, awkward silence.

Well what do you think? I said.

They're not worse. I thought they might get bigger, or itchy, you know?

She was stroking me now, absent-mindedly running her whole hand around the small of my back and a little way along the spine.

How do you feel over all? she asked.

Better. Not so tired. I'll get up anyway.

Mm. Maybe it's good that the sores have come out. Maybe it's like a fever breaking or something.

Maybe.

Coming out to the surface. She sounded almost dreamy now.

I wondered what Christine was looking at, what she was seeing. I couldn't see her, but I could feel the pressure of her knee on the edge of the mattress behind me.

Isn't he hairy? Jenny said, sweeping her hand upwards to my shoulders, and they both laughed. One of them plucked at a hair and they giggled like kids again.

While Christine unpacked in the living room I got out of

bed and dressed, then went up to the bathroom. When I got back down Jenny was telling her about my time on Pugh's farm. It was so sad, she was saying. He was living in a little caravan, all alone except for two mad farmers. When I first met him he could hardly string a sentence together, he was so shy. She laughed, looking at me, then reached out to tug at my hand. Weren't you? she insisted. My little savage. You were like one of those iron age hunters who'd been frozen in the Alps and suddenly got defrosted.

It wasn't so bad, I said, shrugging.

Now he's nearly civilized. He can read and write and everything. She laughed again and I felt myself starting to blush. He still has a bit of trouble shaving though.

It was true – I hadn't felt inclined to shave since falling ill and now my face was hairy as a cat's. Jenny hadn't commented on it until now, but it occurred to me suddenly that underneath the teasing she was disappointed that I hadn't made the effort for Christine. I felt tired, and too warm, and wished I could crawl back onto the bed again. No-one spoke for a while, then Jenny said more seriously: what made you want to go up there in the first place? You never really told me.

Work, I said, surprised by the question. I'd never even asked it myself, even in the middle of the worst nights alone on the hill.

But you could have easily got work in town.

I shrugged again, feeling a little dizzy. I hadn't eaten all day, and maybe because of that the simple, unexpected questions felt confusing in some way. I didn't want to be in town, I said, and tried to smile to cover my awkwardness.

Why? Christine broke in, almost sharply, and suddenly I could feel her eyes on me, intent, anticipating. I opened my mouth but nothing came. Somehow Jenny was excluded now, and this stranger was demanding my attention.

I don't know, I said, and the moment passed, and Jenny started talking about something else, and Christine turned her face politely to listen.

I left them and went through to the bedroom. I felt shaken, as if I'd been on trial and lured to the edge of a confession, and had barely pulled back. I didn't know what the confession would have been, didn't know what had made Christine light up and bear in on me like that, but it left me with a strange, bereft feeling, and I went over to Michael's cot and stared hard at him sleeping there. I wanted to wake him. I had a bad feeling that he was more than asleep, that he was unconscious, in trouble. I pushed the feeling down and moved to the window. There was a breeze picking up off the sea and out beyond the bay a few whitecaps were starting to show. I waited there for a while, taking in the fresh air and waiting for my mood to lift, then closed the window and went back through to the living room.

How's Michael? Jenny asked as I came through. They were both sitting cross-legged on the floor next to the bookcase, facing each other, a pile of children's books between them.

Fine, I said. He's quiet.

You should tell Chris and me some stories about your time on the farm, Jenny said.

I don't have any.

She sniffed. We've been looking at the books we used to read when we were little. I kept them all. She turned back to her sister. Here's the animals book, remember? It was our favourite. We used to fight over it.

She offered it to Christine, who took it but didn't open the cover. It was an old-fashioned children's picture book from the sixties, full of sentimental drawings of puppies, hippy-maned ponies, kittens and so on. She showed it to me not long after we started spending Sunday afternoons in bed together.

Remember when I wrote names under all the animals? I wrote them really artistically I thought. She turned to me. Even though Chris was younger than me, when I showed her what I'd done, really proud, you know, she said it was stupid and I'd ruined the beautiful pictures. Can you imagine? She was only about five, and I was about seven and thought she was bound to be impressed by it. I was stunned. I thought my names were so sophisticated. She laughed and Christine laughed too, but still didn't open the book. She was staring at the big blue kitten on the cover as if trying to recall it, though when Jenny asked her if she remembered it all she nodded confidently.

I gave them all names of drinks, like Brandy and Sherry and Whisky! God, what are kids like?

Christine handed the book back. I remember, she said.

I'm keeping it for Michael, Jenny told her.

Christine went out at four to buy food for the evening meal. Jenny cleaned and fed Michael and sent me to get plates and cutlery from the communal kitchen we shared with our own floor and the next floor up.

On the stairs I passed Clement. He was with a tall, stooping, middle-aged man. They'd just come out of an empty room opposite the stairs at the end of the passage and were talking in Welsh. When he saw me Clement pushed his steel-framed glasses up along the bridge of his nose. He was without his tool bag for once and seemed almost naked – somehow exposed and ridiculous – without it. He knew Christine was visiting and staying a while, and he didn't like it. Not many tenants would ever have wanted what he called his suite though, and we'd taken it long term, so we had some leverage.

Has your visitor arrived then? he asked stiffly, switching to English. I saw a stranger on the stairs just now; I thought it must be her.

That's right, Mr Clement. Arrived this afternoon.

It's as well I know what she looks like.

I agreed.

She seemed quiet enough, anyhow.

No need to worry about that, I said.

No. Well, well, he said. He turned back to the man and I slipped past them and up to the kitchen.

When I came back down they were gone but the door to the room they'd come out of was still wide open. I put my head inside. It was a big square room, well lit by the strong afternoon sun that streamed in through the motes of dust. There was the usual set-up: wash hand basin in the corner, double bed, an old, dark-veneered wardrobe, big as a sarcophagus. I noticed the little list of regulations hanging in a grubby plastic frame near the door. The name of the guesthouse, Bethesda, had been typed into a space left blank for it. So had the numbers for things like breakfast hours, how many people allowed per room, that kind of thing. We'd taken our own list down so long ago I'd forgotten all about it. The image came into my mind of a younger, fresh-faced Clement, full of hopes and plans, typing the same incongruous chapel name into the blanks of each list some twenty or thirty years ago, and suddenly the bright emptiness of the room seemed somehow funereal, like an undertaker's well-lit parlour.

I wondered if he'd been trying to rent it out, or if something needed fixing. Usually when someone new was seeing a room on our floor he'd come and introduce us. He seemed to think it was a nice touch. The only one it ever worked on was Alex, the student teacher. He carried on popping in on us for days after he arrived until I put him straight about it.

I told Jenny about meeting Clement and the stranger while I waited to hand her the plates. She'd opened out the folding table and wanted to improvise a tablecloth from a spare bed sheet before the plates went on it.

If he's moving in, he'd better like the sound of a baby crying, she said.

Jenny was always a little hostile and defensive whenever someone new arrived on our floor: she was convinced that one day soon there would be one too many complaints about the noise Michael made and we'd be forced to move out.

It'll be fine, I said. He was looking at the room at the far end of the corridor, near the stairs. There'd be three other rooms between us.

Michael had woken up for the evening, and once the table was laid I went through to occupy him.

He won't sleep now, Jenny called from the other room. He's already slept more than usual.

I know, I said. I dangled a few toys into the cot, then played hide-and-seek with my face through the bars. He regarded me with a strange, solemn expression. Behind me I heard Christine letting herself in.

Hi, she called. I'm back.

Come and see this, I said over my shoulder.

Still holding the plastic carrier bag she'd come in with, Christine came and stood at my side. I was crouched down, level with her hips.

I pulled a face at him through the bars, ducked away then reappeared in the same spot. Look at his face. Look how serious he is, I said.

Jenny was through now, standing in the doorway watching us.

Look, I said to them both. I've never seen him so serious.

I pulled a face again, but he wasn't looking at me now, he was staring up at Christine.

Christine shifted her stance. He wants to know who I am, she said.

There was quiet for a few seconds.

He's just frightened with you all staring at him, said Jenny, and there was a tightness in her voice. She moved in between myself and Christine and lifted him from the cot. Then she didn't seem to know what to do with him.

I'll take him to the window, I said.

She hesitated. Don't be funny with him, she said. Let him be. Just be nice and peaceful with him.

We stood facing each other. I was conscious of Christine focusing on me again, waiting. Waiting for what?

Come on Jen, I said at last. Give him to me. I'll show him the birds. He likes that. I took him from her.

There wasn't much conversation while we ate. Christine had bought cold Indian food from the corner shop. Some of it was stale and dry but nobody mentioned it. Jenny picked at hers in between fussing with Michael in his high chair. He wasn't eating much either.

How about I go down to the big kitchen and bring up some wine? I said at last. I looked at Jenny and she shrugged.

Is there any left?

A few bottles of that elderflower stuff your mother made. I'll go and see.

Well, it might be nice to have a drink. It might be relaxing.

Christine said nothing.

I'll go then, I said.

The big kitchen was in the basement of the guesthouse and used to be where all the breakfasts and afternoon teas were prepared by the Clements. In fact, you could still book in for half-board and eat in the cellar dining room – it was kept locked but always laid out neatly behind the glass-panelled door, the way ancient tombs were laid out with goblets and bowls all ready for the afterlife – but nobody did that any more as far as we could tell. Instead, the tenants had the use of the basement kitchen, along with the smaller one on the top floor, to cater for themselves. The basement hobs and ovens were filthy but the students living on the lower floors cooked in it without making a fuss. Some of them even ate there, sat together at the long wooden chopping tables like kids in a school canteen.

I managed to get down to the basement without running into Clement again. Their sitting room door was open and I had to go past it to reach the stairs, but their TV was blaring and no one came out.

In the kitchen a couple of students were crouched down at the foot of one of the black industrial-size hobs lining the near wall. They were laughing together, but looked up and nodded when they heard me open the door. One of them was trying to grow a soft little ginger beard. He'd introduced himself to me at some point earlier in the year but I couldn't remember his name. I didn't recognise his friend. I nodded back and stepped through the door.

Luke, man, come and see this roach, the ginger one said.

I went over to where they were squatting. A long black cockroach was labouring around on the tiles between their feet. It had a dod of orange jelly on its back, weighing it down.

We put my mother's home-made marmalade on it, the ginger student explained.

We thought it might dissolve the fucker. They both rocked with silent laughter.

The roach was nearly out of sight now. Its legs were splayed by the extra weight into something like paddles and finally its painfully slow rowing took it to shelter between the feet of the iron hob.

The others might eat it, because of the marmalade, the visitor mused.

The ginger boy snorted.

You've been ages, Jenny complained when I got back with two bottles of wine. Give Christine a hand with the dishes upstairs while I try to get Michael interested in something.

In the smaller upstairs kitchen Christine had finished washing the plates and was inspecting one of the communal tea towels. It was damp and badly stained.

They're all like that, I apologised. Just leave the dishes to drain is the best thing.

She stood for a while, looking around her. She seemed reluctant to head back down. I had the feeling she was waiting for me to go on.

It's just that we share the kitchen, you know? I'll have to show you the kitchen in the basement sometime. It's an experience. I saw the roach again in my mind's eye, its ugly splayed legs dragging its body under the iron range.

She smiled and folded the tea towel neatly before laying it down on the worktop. I passed a man on the stairs when I came up first, she said. Was that the landlord?

A tall guy with white hair? Metal-rimmed glasses?

She nodded. I think so. He had glasses.

That's Clement, I said. He's okay, really. A bit strange, mind.

How do you mean?

Religious strange.

Oh.

When we came looking for rooms he told us we couldn't have them unless we were married. He made me show him the certificate, in fact, though he was good to us after that, once he'd seen it. He might invite you to a Sunday service if he sees you around a bit more. Just about all the tenants get asked. Some of the students actually go.

Have you ever gone with them?

Christ, no.

I felt a faint wave of guilt talking about Clement that way, behind his big, stooped, handyman's back. The truth was he reminded me of my grandfather, and though he made Jenny nervous and impatient, I was always easy, if a little sad, in his company.

She looked around and wiped her palms on her skirt. It was pale blue and full-cut, cool and airy looking. I couldn't remember if it was what she was wearing when she arrived. So what do you believe in? she said abruptly.

I laughed. Nothing much.

Is that why you're unhappy?

I laughed despite myself. I'm not unhappy. What makes you say that?

I can always tell. It's because I work with children. They don't know how to hide things the same way we do, so you learn what to look for.

I'm not unhappy.

She shook her head indulgently and I couldn't help smiling at her self-assurance.

Okay. Well what do you believe in? I asked.

She bowed her head and looked down at her feet for a while, as if summoning up some reserve of strength, or patience. What I believe, she said carefully, is that the living and the dead are just as real as one another, but it's like different languages. Like the way something can be real for two people, but if the language is different you can't talk about it. You can't share it. But it's not that it's not real, it's just not your language. That's the only religious thing I believe now. She finished, a little breathlessly.

I don't think I understand that, I said, startled.

No, she said. I don't expect you to. Though I don't mean anything supernatural, she added, but didn't explain further.

Jenny had warned me that her sister had been brought up very differently to herself after their parents' divorce, and was full of strange ideas. It was their father's fault, she said: he'd run a one-man general practice in Rhondda Fach to begin with, and their early childhood had been conventional enough, but after the separation he'd converted to some tiny Christian sect, quickly becoming its sole voice and authority and using the house as a church for the small congregation. The girls were eleven and nine then, and Christine – who'd always been closer to her father than to Jenny and her mother, 'under his spell' as Jenny put it – insisted on staying with him. For a year or so their mother had fought for custody in the courts, but Christine waged a much fiercer war in return, hardly eating or speaking, taking a scissors to Jenny's clothes more than once, and running away from school to their father at every opportunity. In the end, after two years of chaos, their mother despaired of trying to win her. By then, their father's evangelicalism had hardened into something stranger: he gave up the general practice and opened a centre for spiritual preparation instead: an advance outpost for the second coming. His followers were made up almost entirely of women, some with children, and soon he was running it all in the style of some American ranch cult. There were rumours, of course, about the women and the young girls. When Jenny's mother discovered that he'd made an application to the local authority to educate Christine himself with the help of private tutors, she contacted the social services and the police, making all kinds of accusations. Not long after her fourteenth birthday Christine was taken into care, briefly, but none of the accusations stuck and soon she was back in the big, detached house in Rhondda Fach that had once been the family home, furious and more contemptuous than ever of her mother, and more implacably devoted to her father.

He was twelve months dead now, something Jenny had discovered only in the spring when Christine had broken a silence of ten years to write her a brief letter, and I wondered if her clumsy outburst had simply been her way of invoking him – conjuring him up somehow to be with us – right from the start. I'd already learned from Jenny that she'd left the cult at eighteen to train as a primary school teacher, and in fact the group had fizzled away at about that time until all that were left were one or two of the more desperate and vulnerable hangers-on. But she'd stayed loyal to the man himself if not his beliefs, and had nursed him for a year through the series of heart attacks that weakened and finally killed him.

Christine looked up from studying her feet then and considered me instead for a moment, not meeting my eye but staring hard at my chest in that distant but curious way she had, then laughed freely, as if she'd been playing a game with me all the time. You're much younger than I expected, she announced.

I shrugged, nonplussed.

Let's go back down, she said lightly, and led the way.

Jenny was sitting upright on the edge of the sofa watching TV, a big black and white valve set that Clement had brought up to the room 'to help you keep the little one occupied, see,' soon after we moved in. It had to be thumped into life most evenings, and whined faintly, like a creature, when we switched it off at night. Michael was floundering at Jenny's feet. As I hunted out three wine glasses I heard her explain to Christine that he was learning to crawl.

Where are the bottles? I called through.

In the fridge. Leave them a while to get cold. That wine's no good unless it's cold.

I laid the glasses on the coffee table in front of the TV, then sat on the arm of the sofa next to Jenny. I don't want to wait too long, I said. I'm getting quite tired. I'm not right yet.

I know. I can tell. We won't wait long. She rested her

head against my side.

I shifted my leg to balance the new weight of her leaning against me. I was feeling waves of heat roll over me and the waistband of my jeans was starting to irritate the sores. I put a hand through the buttons of my shirt and tried to ease the rash away from where the denim was pressing. The sores felt more prominent now – small, hard, fiery nubs.

Michael had wormed his way to the low coffee table and was trying to get at the glasses. I leaned forward and pulled him back, which started him grizzling. Leaning forward made me dizzy and I felt a rush of irritation with Jenny for being too absorbed with the TV to shift Michael herself.

What is this anyway? I asked.

It's an old film with Bob Hope. Him and his friend are out of work.

Oh, great.

Well *we're* enjoying it. She looked at her sister for confirmation.

I'm happy, Christine agreed. I like the old black and white films. I like them best.

I was starting to sweat quite freely now, which made the sores around my waist and back itch even more.

Michael was almost at the glasses again. For Christ's sake, Michael, I said and fetched him back more roughly, making him bawl. Keeping hold of his middle I lifted him to my shoulder and carried him through into the bedroom. I sat with him on the bed and talked nonsense and hummed tunes till he'd calmed back down, then gave him my watch to play with. Soon, Jenny brought through his bottle, kissed me on the forehead, and disappeared back to the film while I fed him. He sucked greedily at the teat, staring at my face with grey, wide open eyes until the bottle was empty. It was long past his usual bedtime but he didn't seem sleepy at all.

It's always open season on princesses, Bob Hope told someone. The sun was low now and the weak beams were angled flat across the room. Jenny said something to Christine that I couldn't catch. Soon after I heard the door on the mini-fridge opening and a clink as one of them drew a bottle out. There was quiet for a while. In the movie, a woman with a soft English accent was speaking low and earnestly as if her life depended on what she was saying.

Come back through for some wine, Jenny called. Don't be such a hermit.

The wine, like all the wine Jenny's mother used to make and send us, was cloying even though it had cooled off. It was strong, too, and soon the phases of heat and chill blended into one long, numb sweat. The film ended without my noticing, and soon Jenny and Christine were occupied with Michael and steadily working their way through the last bottle, though it was Jenny doing most of the drinking. The itching around my middle seemed to have stopped, but I kept catching myself gouging at the sores anyway. I felt profoundly sad, but had no idea why.

It was getting dusky in the room before Jenny checked the time. Look at the clock, she said. No wonder Michael's getting grumpy.

I started telling them about the cockroach and the students in the kitchen, but they were so disgusted about there being roaches around the place at all that I couldn't get the story finished. I gave up trying and watched them drink and fool around with Michael. I was remembering my mother from a time when I was six or seven years old – not long after my father had cleared out and a few years before she fell terminally ill. With my father gone we'd moved into a damp, run-down terraced house a few doors down from my grandparents. It was night and I was watching her wipe out a whole colony of roaches – black pats she called them – that had nested behind the fireplace. She'd never have found them except she was having the old Victorian hearth ripped out and getting a gas fire put in. Her brother Roy was doing the heavy work, and he uncovered them. Iesu Grist, Liz, I remember him saying, have a look at this.

I thought she'd be upset because I knew she hated the things, but she was delighted – exhilarated, in fact – and I can still remember the strange, party-like atmosphere that took over our usual gloom. She got Roy to help her boil up the kettle and a few big saucepans of water and I kept watch on the nest, getting a good look at this wonder because I knew it wouldn't be there much longer for me.

It was a winter morning and the roaches were all dormant, plastered to the rotten mortar like a kind of glossy fungus. There were smaller young ones studded among the long slick humps of the adults. I remember longing to touch them, to run a finger over the sleeping smooth bumps, but not daring to wake them. When Roy swept the beam of the torch over their backs they glistened like some Samurai's breastplate of lacquered, black scale armour.

When the water was ready my mother came through, Uncle Roy in tow, and stood me back out of the way. She had thick oven-gloves on and held the heavy steaming kettle out in front of her with both padded hands.

I expected something frantic, but all they did when the water licked over them was drop neatly off and patter into what was left of the grate. It didn't even seem to damage them. It was as if they were being minted into long black coins. When the kettle was done she took a steaming saucepan from Roy and scoured out the last few of them that had found deeper niches in the mortar.

I remember what my mother said to me after Roy had gone. That's the benefit of having family to help you, she told me. You don't have to be ashamed about what you might find.

I don't want any more wine, Christine said at last, and she said it so soberly and definitely that it altered the whole atmosphere.

Jenny looked around and seemed shocked at how quickly the room had darkened. God, it's gloomy all of a sudden, she said.

I'm going to bed, I told them. It's this virus. I don't feel right.

Will you take the cot through? We'll have him in with us, she said to Christine. We normally keep the cot in here, but he'll only wake you.

I wouldn't mind.

No, no, said Jenny.

I dragged the cot after me into the bedroom and set it near the foot of the bed before closing the door behind me. I undressed quickly and got under the covers, desperate to lie down and settle my head. Lying still, I could hear the TV and snatches of their conversation through the wall. It occurred to me that the student teacher could probably hear just as much of our lives every night of the week.

After about half an hour Jenny came through with Michael sleeping in her arms. She put him to bed without a word then crept over to me.

Are you awake?

I grunted.

We're just talking, she slurred. I won't be long. She touched my shoulder with her fingertips. It was very dark in the room. How are you feeling? She bent closer and I could smell the flowery scent of the wine on her breath. She kissed me on the cheekbone. Where are you? she said, and found my lips.

I waited a minute or so after she'd gone back in to Christine, then got out of bed, pulled on my dressing gown and padded out to the corridor and up to the toilet. There was a smell of dope in the air around the bathroom, but it was faint and could have come from anywhere. Inside, standing in front of the mirror, I had a good look at the sores. Some of them were ugly where I'd scratched them, a map of angry red blotches banding my stomach. I splashed my face and some of the rash with cold water before going back down.

I don't know how long Jenny and Christine stayed up talking. I know Jenny would have been trying to fill in a lot of blank space. I don't know what Christine wanted. Jenny had explained to me the week before Christine arrived that now their father was dead things would go better between them. I thought I'd lost my only sister for life, I remember Jenny telling me in the days before Christine arrived. I thought I'd never know or care if she lived or died. Can you imagine that; your own sister? Your own family?

I thought I could imagine it, but didn't say so.

Now, while they talked, I drifted in and out of sleep,

escaping in a sweat from nightmares, then falling back into them. All I remember now about the dreams is the figure of Jenny's father. He was dead, I understood in the dream, though there was nothing to show it. He was trying to tell me something, calling to me from a small round window high up in a blank wall. One moment it was his face, the next moment he was using Christine's, at the same window, white and expressionless. When her lips moved I was suddenly awake and listening to the murmurings through the wall, the blood knocking in my head.

At some point during the long night Jenny came to bed. Even in the state I was in I could sense her happiness and excitement. She lay close and trapped my feet with her own, then she moved a foot up and down my shin. The soles of her feet were deathly cold.

Don't Jen, you're freezing, I murmured. Her feet must be white, it occurred to me, like Christine's face in the dream. I'm asleep, I said.

She chuckled. No you're not. Let me talk.

I gasped as she slid an icy palm between my legs. I eased an arm free and hooked it behind her head on the pillow.

I'm so happy she's here, she whispered. It's like a miracle. We get on just like old friends. She paused for a while and I could hear her breathing. I thought he'd robbed me for life. I never told you, but it used to make me so lonely. I hated him. I hated him for it.

Just before I fell back into sleep I remember her lifting her head from the pillow and insisting, I want you to like Chris. I want you both to get on. We're all family now. I've forgiven her everything.

I nodded.

Now he's gone, I've got so much hope for her.

I could sense her staring hard at the side of my face and was suddenly afraid to turn and make eye contact. I could smell the wine on her breath again.

Do you like her? I know you haven't had much time, but do you think you'll like her? Do you think you could love her like a sister? She nudged me and clasped her frozen feet around mine. Luke? she said.

I'm sure I'll like her, I said, drugged with sleep, wanting nothing more than to fall away into the dark, away from this strange interrogation.

I hope so. That's what I really hope.

Me too, then, I mumbled. That's what I hope too.

★

Over the next few days the virus got worse and I spent most of the time in the flat, either exhausted in bed or looking after Michael while Jenny took Christine around the town. To begin with I tried to keep working my shifts at the warehouse – I had no chance of sick-pay – but as it took hold of me harder I could barely get up the stairs to the bathroom without resting, so I called Anzani and told him I wouldn't be in for what was left of the week. Jenny was pleased, despite the lost money: it meant she could use up the last of her holiday leave spending time with Christine, who still had a full month before term started again. She was teaching then in a small prep school outside Cardiff, and sometimes spent a few hours after breakfast preparing, with child-like concentration, meticulous, colourful lesson plans and projects for her classes – The

World Inside a Rock Pool, An Octopus's Garden, Selkies and Mermaids – though as it turned out she would never get the chance to use them.

The weather stayed fine, the usual cool summer wind blowing in from the sea most days until evening, then everything growing calm again and the rooms of the guesthouse glowing in the rays of the setting sun. Sometimes Jenny would take Christine out on a bus trip and they'd go inland to little market towns or along the coast to better beaches. At the end of Christine's first week they went all the way to Swansea, leaving on the early bus and getting back after dark.

At 6 every morning Christine slipped out quietly, made her way to the far end of the beach in the shadow of Constitution Hill and swam, on calm days, for at least thirty minutes around the headland and back. The first time, Jenny – incredulous, and convinced the currents would sweep her away – insisted on us taking Michael and watching her from the rocks, ready to run for a telephone at any sign of trouble. Christine laughed at her sister's concern but said she didn't mind if we really wanted to trail along and be bored. She swam a slow, smooth breast-stroke that looked steady enough to carry her all the way to America if she'd wanted. At the furthest point from land she trod water for a time, the dark speck of her head motionless and barely visible against the gunmetal grey of the water. Why isn't she moving? Jenny asked. What's she doing out there? Maybe she's got cramp and can't swim any more. But after a minute or so the tiny paleness of her face began dipping and reappearing again, and we knew she was coming back to us.

In the middle of Christine's second week, on the

Wednesday or Thursday morning, I woke feeling much stronger, as if the virus had lifted its siege quite suddenly in the night. Jenny was already up and through in the living room with Michael. I heard her ask Christine if she wanted a coffee and realised she must have already come back from her swim. The first sharp nappy smell of the day drifted through and there was the sound of a new bag of disposables being popped open. Can you hold him just there? Jenny was saying.

I waited a while before getting up, wondering if the new energy I felt was just temporary or would stand my moving around. I was dizzy when I bent to step into my jeans, but apart from that I felt fine. Even the scabs left by the sores had grown paler overnight and were drying up.

They were both surprised to see me when I went through. Christine was wearing a big white T-shirt she obviously used as a nightdress. Her hair was still wet from showering after her swim. I hadn't seen her in anything like bedclothes before – she'd always been up and dressed before me. Now she seemed awkward at my being there. She was kneeling at Michael's head, distracting him while Jenny changed the nappy and cleaned him, and when I came and stood over them she took hold of the front hem of her T-shirt and pulled it so it tucked under her knees. Look who it is, she said to Michael. It's your daddy.

Hello honey, Jenny said, glancing up. She finished wiping around Michael's thighs, then powdered him. Feeling a bit better?

Much better.

Good. I'm glad. Chris, can you take this out of the way? She handed the talcum powder to Christine.

I wouldn't mind getting some fresh air today, I said.

There was silence, except for the pat-pat of Jenny's hand on each tiny buttock. Michael sneezed.

Had you two planned to go anywhere?

No, I don't think there's anywhere else you really want to see is there? Jenny asked Christine.

We've done plenty of shopping for a while, Christine said. I've spent too much anyway.

You haven't bought much, Jenny laughed. I end up buying things though. I'm just weak. She rolled Michael onto his back and fastened the front of his nappy. Are you going to go back to work? she asked me.

I should, I said. I'll go into town and see how I feel. I could do the afternoon shift.

I didn't mean you should. Don't if you still feel tired. I was only joking when I said I'd been buying stuff.

I'd better get something on, said Christine. I'm the only one not dressed. She ran a hand through her hair. What a mess, she said. I keep forgetting to dry it properly.

You're on holiday, Jenny said, you're allowed to be a mess. Anyway, it's just family.

I felt too hot outside wherever there was shelter from the wind – I was still a little feverish – but I was glad to be out in the open at last.

I decided to walk the mile or so to the university library. I'd been able to take out an associate membership because of my OU registration, and I wanted some history books for the module I was studying. I'd fallen behind while I was ill. There was a back way from the seafront to the campus, not much more than a track which climbed steeply through woods, skirted a few long fields and then opened out near the top of the campus hill at a big greenhouse used by the

Botany department. I found myself needing to rest more than once on the first sharp climb away from the sea, but once the path levelled out it was pleasant to make my way along the edge of the open fields, listening to the ripening barley whisper and shush in the breeze.

Outside the library I heard my name called and turned to find Bill Kerrigan striding towards me, grinning and shading his wide, bearded face from the sun with a big hand. Kerrigan was an old student friend of Jenny's – I always suspected they'd been together for a short time before I met her, which turned out to be correct – and because he'd stayed on to do a PhD rather than dispersing along with most the rest of their circle they'd stayed fairly close. Sometimes he visited the guesthouse to eat and get drunk with us. I liked him: he was vague, shy and shambling – he looked at least ten years older than he was – and rarely spoke unless he had something worthwhile to say. He'd been interested in the farm and had even gone away to research it after I'd told him about my time there. It went back to the fourteenth century, he discovered. The farmhouse had been extended a little in Victorian times, but its dark, low-ceilinged kitchen and living room were medieval.

Luke, he said, still grinning and shading his eyes. Haven't seen you in a while.

We swapped news for a short time and I told him about Christine's visit. He nodded, frowning, as if trying to recall something. Jenny used to talk about her sometimes, he said at last. When she was drunk. I'm surprised she's visiting.

I think Jenny was surprised too, I said. But it's going fine, I think.

He seemed to mull it over for a moment, then said: bring

her to a party, if you like. I mean if you want something to do with her. Next Wednesday at my place.

Ok, I said, if we can get a sitter for Michael.

He scratched his beard, still looking thoughtful. See you there then, maybe, he said, and waved a hand as he turned toward the library steps.

I managed to get through the afternoon at the warehouse without too much strain: Anzani had drafted one of his sons in to cover for me being away so I actually had had some help for once when the drivers called in to get their vans loaded. By five o'clock I was exhausted though: I'd eaten almost nothing when the fever was bad and now I realised my muscles were running on empty. None of the shipments were particularly heavy, but I was drenched with sweat. You ok? You look like you're having a heart attack, Anzani's boy said as we finished the last load.

I nodded, but hardly had the energy to reply.

You look like shit. I mean it, he said.

Back at Bethesda Mrs Clement was perched in her rocking chair in the big bay window, slightly above pavement level, overlooking the prom. She was a big, iron-haired woman who liked to spend the whole day there behind glass, knitting or sewing, and watching the world go by with a fixed, aghast look, as if it were all some kind of slowly unfolding atrocity that she couldn't take her eyes off. She watched me crossing the street from the bus stop but when I looked up to acknowledge her she stared straight out to sea, pretending she hadn't noticed me at all. Inside, their flat door was closed for once and there was no sound coming from its living room.

Jenny and Christine were out somewhere with Michael. I looked for a note but there wasn't any. I knew I needed to eat, but at the same time couldn't face the thought of swallowing anything down. I drew the curtains in the living room and slumped in a corner of the sofa.

I was still there when they got back. They'd had a good afternoon, Jenny told me, and Michael was so tired now he'd sleep all evening. She didn't say where exactly they'd been but I supposed it must have been a long walk around town, or maybe along the bay.

I felt almost too tired to speak, but told Jenny about meeting Kerrigan and the invitation to his party.

Do you want to go? she asked.

I shrugged.

I don't want to, she said, but I could stay with Michael and you could take Christine. Do you think he'd mind?

I shrugged, feeling stung that Jenny thought he might not want me there if I wasn't with her.

Do you want to go to a party? she asked her sister.

That would be nice, she said, looking at me.

Well, it must be boring for you in the nights, because of Michael, Jenny said. It'll be a change.

Four

I was woken the next morning by Michael's weight settling on my stomach. Jenny laughed when I opened my eyes.

Don't move, she said, you'll tip him off.

I waited, letting him crawl up onto my chest, letting his little fist dig unsteadily at my windpipe. He rested there.

Give daddy a kiss, she told him.

I worked an arm free from under the sheets and rolled him into it, cupping him there.

Let me see your waist, Jenny said, and knelt on the bed at my side. She hauled down the sheets and examined me. Look how pale they've gone, she said. They look a lot better.

I craned my neck to see. She was right – except for the ones I'd mauled with my fingernails, the pock marks were hardly noticeable now.

Do you still feel better?

I nodded from the pillow.

Good. Let's go out today. We could take Chris along the cliff path. Do you feel strong enough for that?

I'll be fine. I told Anzani I'd work an afternoon shift today though.

She nodded. That's ok. We'll start out early and get back. I want you to have some time with her too. I want you to get to know each other. She looked hard at me, as if measuring me up for the task ahead. She's not back from her swim yet. You could get dressed while she's gone. She bent forward and lifted Michael away.

It had been quite a while – more than a year, I suppose – since we'd climbed Constitution Hill together to get to the cliffs, and now when we reached the top we rested on the steps of a new, ugly cafe that had been rigged up there since the last time. It was just a low, flat-roofed hut of weatherproofed boards, and some were already starting to warp and split in the rough sea air. It wasn't open yet and there was no sign of life through the windows inside. I was carrying Michael in his sling on my back; despite the sharp breeze I was sweating and glad to catch my breath.

I didn't know this was here, Jenny said. It must be to go with the camera obscura.

Christine stood up and wandered over to a crude chipboard signpost which read: Opening Soon – Britain's Biggest Camera Obscura. There was a heap of building materials lying just beyond it. They'd been there longer than the cafe – I remembered seeing them the last time we'd been here. Then we'd taken the funicular railway up the slope because Jenny was far gone in the pregnancy and not confident of climbing, though for some reason she'd felt in the mood for a stroll along the cliffs. I remember the spring weather turning suddenly, a squall of hailstones battering in off the sea, and Jenny trying to hurry back along the path, clutching her big stomach.

Is this where it's going to be? Christine called.

We both shrugged.

She stepped into the midst of the bricks and steel spines and peered down at them as if the big, spying mirror was already in place there.

Jenny put her arm out behind me and tickled Michael.

He likes being carried, doesn't he, she said to me over my shoulder. He looks so funny though, doesn't he, staring out backwards at everything.

I didn't answer. Jenny always wanted Michael to sit facing forwards when I carried him, and that was how the harness was meant to go, but the first few times we tried it he got ever more hysterical the longer the walk went on, hitting out at the back of my head. I don't know what gave me the idea of turning him round, but it worked, and he was immediately calm. When I was young I used to get anxious facing forwards in trains – I preferred seeing everything slipping away to seeing everything coming at me headlong – so maybe it was something we shared.

That sign's been up for more than a year, Jenny called across to her sister. And all those bricks and things, she added. They must have run out of money, or changed their minds.

Slowly Christine turned and picked her way back to us. The wind was gusting in over the lip of the cliff behind us, directly into her face. Her mouth, tensed against the breeze, seemed to be smiling at some secret.

We carried on, filing away from the empty cafe and onto the path, following its curve away from the cliff-edge and into a stretch of sheltering gorse and bracken. Jenny was walking ahead of me, Christine behind, and when we climbed up out of the bushes, back onto bare rock and into the teeth of the wind again, I remember Jenny glancing back, suddenly fearful, to check that Michael was still safe behind my shoulders, as if he might have been plucked free and flung out onto the water far below.

We'd been walking for nearly half an hour when Michael started crying. For a while I ignored it – it didn't sound urgent, just bad-tempered. Jenny was still in front, too far ahead to hear him. It went on for about ten minutes before I felt something sting the back of my ear. I stopped and turned and out of the corner of my eye saw a fragment of grit drop from my shoulder to the ground. At that moment Christine drew level and looked me in the face as she passed. Her eyes were shining, as if she were bristling with an electric pleasure and energy. Without slowing or taking her eyes from mine she reached out swiftly and touched my ear where the tiny stone had hit it. Then she was in front of me, breaking into a run to catch up with Jenny.

For a few minutes I followed after them mechanically. Then I stopped, loosened the straps of Michael's sling, sat down against the grass bank on the landward side of the path and eased my arms free. Sure enough, when I turned him round I could see a clutch of tiny, sharp-edged stones nestled in a fold of his bib. They were dark grey and flinty, the same rock as the cliffs. I checked his face but there were no marks. He was still sobbing but the edge had gone from it. He was just feeling sorry for himself now. I cleared the grit away, then swung him back behind my shoulders and tightened the straps again. I don't know why, but I didn't feel angry or protective; all I could think of was the lit expression on her face as she passed and the touch of her finger on me, like a blessing.

By the time I secured the sling and started walking again Jenny and Christine were almost out of sight, winding their way down the incline to Clarach, the first bay beyond the town. I watched their heads bob down below the ridge, Christine's dark hair burnished by the morning sun.

Once they reached the sand they turned together, as

if in silent agreement, and waited while I worked my way down toward them. The tide was out but there were no birds on the sand, just a distant armada of gulls resting on the swells in the bay. Michael was quiet again now and the whole vista, from the far off gulls to the rock under my feet, seemed unnaturally still. I had a sudden sense of being suspended above the landscape, pinned in space by the attention of the women below me. Then Jenny put up her hand to wave and broke the spell, and Christine turned away to the sea.

Smile, Jenny said when I finally reached her. She grinned, showing me what she meant.

How far do you want to go?

She looked over to where Christine was standing; she'd wandered out of earshot from us. I don't know, Jenny said. I think she's enjoying it.

We could go on to the village, I suggested. We could get some food. I wouldn't mind sitting down a while.

Is Michael getting heavy?

A bit, I lied. Really all I wanted was to get my thoughts together. Or did I want to see Christine's face again, as closely as I saw it when she reached out to touch me?

Let's do that then. We could show her the old church.

I hitched Michael higher, ready to carry on.

At the far side of the bay two dogs were rushing towards the breakers. A faint bark carried down on the wind. They tumbled heavily into each other and as they rolled apart their owner appeared out of the shadow of the cliffs.

Give Christine a call, I said. She's almost at the water.

I'll run and get her. You go on and we'll catch you up. She went round to my back and chattered for a moment with Michael before setting off. I turned once and saw

Jenny running quickly and lightly as a girl, almost skipping, and Christine, facing her now, unmoving at the sea's edge.

The village church stands at a crossroads behind the bay. Eastward the road runs away from the sands and on up the broad valley behind the beach. It's a modern road, built mainly for a caravan park set up between two sandy bays on drained flatlands. North and south it follows a much older route, linking all the coastal settlements for miles and focusing them on the church. To one side of the crossroads there's a general store which sells beach toys, newspapers, sandwiches and ice-creams. On the other side a few low cottages cluster round a stone footbridge spanning the brook. The clear, stony spate-stream, just a trickle by the end of summer, is all that's left of whatever Ice Age torrent once filled the valley. It's a peaceful place even when the caravan park gets busy in high season. There's no pub or cafe, and most of the tourists head for town, or for the bigger beach further north where the swimming is safer.

I bought some filled rolls and tins of Coke from the store and took everything over to a bench near the brook. I eased Michael's sling off my back but kept him sat in the harness, settling the whole structure against the arm and back-rest of the bench. He seemed happy with that.

There was no sign of Jenny and Christine so I wandered onto the stone bridge and watched an old man and a little boy fishing in the shade there. The ankle-deep water was very clear and smooth and every piece of gravel on the stream bed was bright as a gem under the currents. It must have been hopeless for fishing, but the old man was humouring the kid, pointing out where he should be steering the bait. I followed the line of his finger and there was the worm, hanging in the flow. It looked bleached out but still had the strength to loop against the hook every so often.

Keep him tight in now, the man said. There was a wheeziness in his voice, and occasionally he would cough from deep in his lungs and his whole body would shake. It didn't seem to bother the boy though. He must have been used to it.

The boy tugged the rod and threadline back and ran the worm back down a fresh strip of gravel, this time closer in to the bank. It trundled over the stones until the line tightened and swung up against the current again.

Tight in. That's right, that's the boy. Get him in the shade there.

Is he in the shade now?

He's fine now. Keep him tight in. That's where you want him.

There wasn't any shade that I could see. Even right in at the banks there was no overhang, just one long bright strip of sand and pebbles and gravel under the sun.

Over the bridge, in the garden of one of the cottages, a slow-moving old woman had started hanging out her washing. Can you mind the banks if you have to fish there? she said, eyeing the boy suspiciously. They'll be washed away, see, if the grass gets loosened.

He's minding the bank all right, the old man answered. The boy glanced up at her, his mouth slack and innocent-looking. He shuffled his feet back an obedient few inches from the water's edge.

She finished hanging out the clothes. There were just two shirts and a bed sheet. Some things she left in the basket. She stared at the boy's back for a while, then shuffled indoors.

The old man watched her go. Get him tight in again, that's the boy, he said, but you could tell his heart wasn't in it now.

Shall I try a spinner? the boy asked.

You could try a spinner. He nodded carefully, as if contemplating this, but his eyes were wandering away from the water now, taking in the sky, the garden opposite and finally me, on the bridge, looking down at them.

I like spinners better than worms.

Well then. Let's try a spinner, is it?

A finger tapped me on the shoulder and I turned.

Hello stranger, Christine said. The old man looked up again and for the first time the boy realised he was being watched and craned to face us too. I tried to think of some reply, but couldn't.

Any luck? Christine called down brightly to the boy.

No, no luck, the old guy answered for him. He nodded at us.

I had a bite but it might have been a stone, the boy piped.

We left them and sat with Jenny and Michael on the bench. Food's in the bag, I said. Just some rolls.

Jenny handed them out and we started eating. It was warm in the sun and easy to sit there without speaking, savouring the sunshine and the cool sea breeze.

I heard the old man say something about the tide, then the sound of the boy reeling in his line drifted up from near the bridge.

You could take Christine to see the church while I feed Michael, Jenny suggested. I was telling her about the carvings on the way up from the beach. Among other things. She leaned forward and grinned at her sister. A cool smile ghosted onto Christine's lips, but her eyes were closed, lids angled to the sun like petals.

Don't you want to go yourself?

I don't mind. It's something for you to do while he's fed. She looked at me meaningfully, as if I was missing something.

I looked across at Christine again. Her eyes were open now but seemed unfocused, disinterested. The roll she was eating was less than half finished but she slipped it back into the carrier bag anyway and brushed a few crumbs off her jeans. She took a light sip from her can, then set it down on the bench and said she was ready.

Neither of us spoke on the way to the church, though when we got to the porch she asked me to wait while she read through a dog-eared booklet which gave some information about the building. When she was done I lifted the heavy black latch and we stepped in.

I found out about the carvings in the church not long after moving out to Pugh's farm. I'd walked along the cliffs one cool, lonesome Sunday afternoon and discovered the bay and then the church behind it. An old caretaker was inside, working on one of the iron radiators. When he saw me staring at the woodwork on the pulpit, he called me over to the choir stalls. If you like carvings, look at these now, he said, and pointed out a series of narrow ledges, half-seats set in the shadows of the backmost row. The stall, almost hidden behind the others, was clearly much older than the rest of the furniture in the place. The wood was smoother and darker and made on a smaller scale than the rows in front of it. Nearly a thousand years old, he said, full of satisfaction. Saved from the abbey at Strata Florida, see.

The ledges were decorated with chunky, stylized carvings of people and animals. Take a good look, he said. Take your time, if you like that kind of thing. He went back to work on the radiator.

What are they? I asked.

Misericords, he answered over his shoulder. Mercy seats. They were made for the really old monks so they could rest their arses when the prayers went on too long.

Most of the carvings showed animal scenes – a fox preaching to geese; a monkey playing a cat through its tail like bagpipes; pigs tearing a wolf to pieces with bizarre, dagger-like fangs; a grinning dog parting a monk's habit with his huge head and jaws, clamping its teeth on his genitals. The farthest was shadowed in the corner of the stall and hard to make out: a fish arched over what looked like flames and a human figure beating an ape with a staff.

The church was one of the first places I took Jenny when we started seeing each other. She'd found it hilarious that my idea of a date was showing her such odd, grotesque things, and it became one of our few private jokes together. Part of me resented sharing it with Christine now, but I was excited, too, by a creeping sense of symmetry in it all. I'd had a powerful feeling of déjà vu as she crouched to examine the pictures, and I moved away from her and sat down in one of the pews to let the sensation pass. It seems odd to me now that I didn't confront her about the pellets of grit in Michael's sling. It was still on my mind, of course, and I half intended to bring it up when we were alone in there, but she hadn't harmed him as such, and she'd shown no sign of guilt or embarrassment, so I suppose I didn't know how to begin. And I was curious more than angry. It was as if I couldn't ask her that question while there were other, much simpler but much more difficult, questions between us.

Why are the pictures so violent? she said, her voice muffled behind the stalls.

They're fables. All the animals are symbols for things.

Like what?

Devils and demons, priests, Jews, lust, Christ. All that kind of thing.

How do you know about all that?

I read up on them. They're from an old abbey about twenty miles away. But there are others all around the country. All around Europe, in fact.

Were they stolen?

Well, the abbey's just a ruin. Someone must have saved them. They were in another church for a few hundred years before they were moved here.

They're good, she said flatly, then stood up straight again and let her gaze wander round the whole church. They're so childish, in a way, she added. It's funny.

I waited, expecting her to carry on, but she just folded her arms and half leaned, half sat against the back of one of the pews.

I looked up at the modern stained glass windows: cheery, inoffensive pastels in abstract organic shapes. I felt Christine at my elbow, though I hadn't noticed her moving towards me.

Dad was always dragging us off to look at church windows, she said. Real ones though, not like these.

You and Jenny? I asked.

All of us, she said. It was his idea of a good day out.

Driving halfway across the country to gawk at some old glass. It used to drive Jennifer and my mother crazy, she added. It was the first time I'd ever heard anyone refer to Jenny by her full name, but Christine spoke so flatly it was impossible to guess at any feeling behind her words. Just for an instant my dream came back to me: their father's face at a high window, staring down at me, mouthing, becoming Christine. It was a face I'd only ever seen in a photograph, and then only briefly before Jenny shuffled it away again. He hated organised religion, she went on. It drove him wild, but he loved looking inside churches. He never told us why, or what we should like about them too. He was a complicated man. I feel like I'll never really understand him. Nobody did.

Did you like seeing them?

She smiled and shrugged.

I wanted to ask more about the family, but didn't know how to go about it without embarrassing us both.

Did Jennifer tell you that our father committed suicide?

In my surprise I almost laughed. It wasn't so much the idea of suicide as the idea of Jenny keeping it from me that seemed absurd. I had no idea what to say. In the end I said a simple no, but kept enough surprise in my voice to prompt more information.

What did she tell you?

Heart disease, I said, truthfully. She told me you'd nursed him for a while, at the end.

She sniffed. At the end, she repeated, then strode over to one of the windows and glared at it.

I cleared my throat. I remember the dry, false sound it made in the dead air. The last time I'd come here there was rotting fruit all over the windowsills, I remembered. It was some weekday after Harvest Festival and the weather had turned hot and humid. Dozens of slow, droning wasps were weaving back and forth, shuttling from window to window as if carrying cargo. It had seemed almost dreamlike; the big, drowsy wasps and the yellow sun pouring onto them through the glass.

They killed him, really, she said. They hounded him into illness, then into his grave. All their lies. They didn't know anything, but they said they did. They tried to make me turn against him, like a Judas. There wasn't the slightest tremor of passion in her voice. It would have been less unnerving, less frightening, in fact, if there had been. It wasn't any of their business, his life, she went on in the same low, disengaged tone, and they killed him.

Who did? I said, knowing I was being obtuse, but wanting to respond in some way that would keep her talking. Jenny and her mother? The sound of a big vehicle driving by on the road outside filtered in through the stained glass. A tractor, I thought. The engine had the same throaty pitch and rhythm as the old Massey Ferguson on Pugh's farm.

These windowsills are filthy, she said at last. I want to go out now.

I didn't reply, but she turned anyway and waited for me to start back toward the door.

Jenny was sitting on the graveyard wall with her back to us. She was holding Michael upright and he was staring over her shoulder at Christine as she approached. Along the road I could see the boy and the old man wandering away from the bridge, trailing their fishing gear. The boy held the rod low and carelessly behind him and with each step the rod flexed a little and the tip kissed the road with a whispered tsk.

Jenny asked Christine if she'd liked the church and the carvings, explaining some of the things I'd already told her about them, but Christine didn't give any sign, she just let Jenny talk. It made me vaguely sad and irritable. I went through the wicket gate into the churchyard and sat on the warm stone wall, listening to Jenny carrying on her monologue to Christine. When she finished there was silence except for birdsong out of the cemetery, the wind in the tops of the yew trees, and the occasional distant screech of a gull. The fact that we were sat at a crossroads seemed to make the emptiness more desolate than peaceful. I found myself wondering how old the roads might be; the drovers' route into the hills and the coastal way running north and south past farmhouses dotted on headlands and empty shingle beaches. There were heat shimmers rippling off the road now where the man and the boy had disappeared. I thought of questioning Christine again, and wondered if a chance would come now before she left. What are you doing here? I wanted to say. What is it you want?

Luke?

I realised that the two of them were standing beside the wall now, waiting for me to move.

Ok? Jenny asked.

I nodded and pushed myself forward off the fat stone lip.

Can you hold him while I put the sling on you? I want to make sure it's fastened right.

I held Michael and turned for Jenny as she clipped the straps into place around my shoulders and chest, tugging them tighter than they'd been. It's like saddling a horse, she said, then lifted Michael from me and slotted him in.

Gee up, she said, and smacked a buttock. Let's go across the beach to the caves. We've got time before your shift starts. There's a smuggler's cave, she said to Christine. We can go past it on the way back.

The wind had freshened and was whipping into our faces each time we turned seawards. The dogs I'd seen earlier were still around but they'd stopped playing and were quartering the wide beach now, noses to the sand. They worked separately, though every so often one would glance up unerringly at the other, however far apart they'd wandered. Their owner was stood some way ahead of us in the shelter of the cliffs, smoking and gazing out into the bay. As we drew near him the dogs came bounding in from their patrols, tongues lolling. The first to arrive, a heavy black Labrador, made straight for Michael. He reached me, panting, and lunged up, balancing on his hind legs, his paws scraping the back of my arm.

Hey! Stop that! I heard Jenny yell, but there was nothing fierce in its big, dull face.

I turned and pushed it back with my forearm, but it kept its balance and a warm string of saliva swung onto my wrist as it jostled to stay upright. Get off, I ordered, pushing again, and this time it gave way and let its sandy forepaws drag down along my body to the ground.

Don't worry, the owner called over to us, he's just wondering if it's food you've got.

Well it's bloody well not. It's a baby, Jenny snapped back.

He strode toward us, raising a hand to pacify Jenny, and winked at me.

Jenny was at the dog's flank now, urging it from us. Go on, piss off, she was hissing, but the dog just nuzzled her thighs, then spun away and jumped up at my back again.

Luther! The man intervened at last, yanking it down by its collar. Come away.

It loped off, reluctant, and joined the other dog, a German Shepherd, which had ignored us and was nosing around the debris washed up under the cliffs. Good boy, the owner enthused, then turned to apologise. Too friendly by half, isn't he? He lifted his hand again in a kind of wave, a stubby cigar lodged between its fingers. Jenny muttered something that sounded far from friendly back but I couldn't make out the words.

Christine had carried on ahead of us, and by the time Jenny had finished checking Michael over and I'd finished wiping the drool off my wrist with a dod of damp sand, she was out of sight behind a tall outcrop. Jenny was still cursing the dog and its owner, but I wasn't listening.

As we rounded the outlying rocks Christine was already returning from the small inlet it concealed. It wasn't really much of a cave – more just a fissure in the rocks. Most of it was open to the sky though a few big boulders had broken off the cliff and wedged high up, partly roofing the sand and strips of kelp below.

Any pirate gold? I asked her, wanting to slow her down and bring her alongside us.

She nodded a fraction. Go and see, she said.

Jenny began to follow me but Christine called her back. Come to the rock pools with me, she told her, and set off quickly so that Jenny had to break into a jog to catch up.

The air inside the inlet smelled salty and rotten. Fresh graffiti had been spray-painted white on a slab of dark stone near the back of the cavity: the outline of a couple fucking. The woman was on her hands and knees, the man also on his knees but upright behind her. Though just a crude outline it was done unusually well – every line, from the tilt of her neck to the curve of her buttocks nested in his groin seemed accurate in a way that made my stomach fold. I thought of Christine looking at it; lips parting just a little maybe, the white of her teeth behind them. Go and see.

I found them both in the lee of the next promontory, standing over something in the sand, Christine teasing it with the toe of her plimsoll. They both glanced up as I came near.

Look, said Jen, and pointed at the sand.

Christine kept her eyes fixed on me, and her face wore the same triumphant expression I'd seen earlier on the cliff-path. There was something childlike in her pleasure, which made it seem worse. It was a relief to stare down at whatever it was Jenny wanted me to see.

It's a skate, she said. Look at the length of it. She was still pointing and now with her fingertip she traced the long whip of its tail bones. The skeleton was half sunk into the coarse sand, a few shreds of grey, leathery skin still clinging to the ribs.

Look at the teeth, said Christine, though now she was playing with Michael behind my back. I felt him wriggling in his seat. Towards or away from her? I wondered.

There was something prehistoric-looking about the skull of the fish. The bared teeth seemed out of proportion to the rest of the head. They lay flat in the open jaws like cased knives and their flatness reminded me of the teeth in the carvings. The biggest were over an inch long. I thought of the Labrador jumping at Michael's soft legs. He was moving at my back again, keening out an unfamiliar sound.

Don't do that to him, Jenny said, an edge in her voice which I hadn't heard her use with her sister before.

She joined Christine behind me. He didn't like that, she murmured. Then: Let me wipe you, she said to Michael. Keep still for me. Good boy.

Was it here we found the seal? I asked her over my shoulder.

I heard Jenny's lips smack a kiss on Michael's head. That's right, she said. I'd forgotten about that. It was up against the rocks, she told Christine, just back from here I think.

Christine didn't respond.

At first we thought it was a body, Jenny went on, ignoring her sister's silence. It looked like a man in a wet overcoat, hunched up, didn't it, Luke? And we could smell that it was dead. I didn't want to look and find out.

I nodded, remembering. When I'd first seen the big, sodden heap, the rain tapping on the dark hump of its shoulders, I'd been convinced it was human. It seemed inevitable, somehow.

We got caught in a storm that day, Jenny said, to no one in particular. In the end we had to shelter in the cave from lightning. She finished adjusting Michael and moved alongside me, slipping a hand into mine.

Let's go back, Christine said, and started walking.

Five

I hung back and let Jenny and Christine go on ahead of me for most of the walk back along the cliffs from Clarach. Now and then they paused and I watched them exchange a few words, but for the most part we trudged on in single file and I was glad to be left to my own thoughts. I left Michael with them at the door to Bethesda and carried on to the warehouse, taking the longer way past the pier and the cormorants drying their wings on the black rocks beside it.

A couple of big deliveries were due and once they arrived the time passed quickly. Most of my tiredness from the days before seemed to have passed and it was calming to tick off the delivery sheets, stacking the boxes onto the hand truck and wheeling them into their places. Anzani's son slipped away with nothing more than a nod soon after I arrived, and apart from the drivers I worked alone.

By the time I got home the sun was already westering and facing full on to Bethesda, filling the sitting room with warm yellow blocks of light. Jenny was sitting slumped on the sofa, Michael awake but peaceful in her arms. She looked up and smiled. Can you take him for a while? she said. I lifted him free and settled him against my shoulder. Where's Christine? I asked.

She went upstairs to take a bath. Jenny closed her eyes, laid her head against the armrest of the couch and yawned. She hardly said a word to me on the way back.

No. Nor to me.

I tried to get her talking, but it was no good. Maybe she's just tired. It must be strange for her, spending time with me now after so many years. I know it's strange for me.

I almost spoke, but didn't.

The sea air makes you tired too if you're not used to it, she said drowsily. She yawned again and seemed to think for a while, her eyes still closed. Do you think she's bored? she went on at last.

No, just tired, I said. You're right. It must be strange for her.

She nodded and opened her eyes at last. We'll take her out tonight. Just for a quiet drink. Is that a good idea? Do you think she'd like that? Even if she's tired? It might help her to relax. I think she gets tense being inside all evening. She must feel like she's on show or something.

It would be something to do, I agreed.

We'll get Mrs Clement to look after Michael. She'll like that. Then Jenny was quiet again for a time. We were both waiting for Christine. I had a strong impulse to yawn, just as a way of feigning normality and indifference. The door to the hall was open and the sound of a radio was drifting up the stairs from one of the students' rooms below ours. My mouth is so dry, said Jenny.

I'll get a drink, I said.

Will you pour one for Chris, too? She'll be down soon.

Without meaning to we all slept until dusk, as if the late sunshine pouring through the window had drugged us – Jenny cradling Michael on the sofa, myself bolstered on cushions next to her and Christine upright in the armchair.

I woke first, disorientated by the new, cool twilight. There was a faint whistling from either Jenny's nostrils or Michael's, but otherwise no sound at all. I looked across through the gloom at Christine. Her ankles were crossed at the foot of the chair, her knees parted, her hands folded in the lap of her denim skirt. She seemed almost to be meditating. I got up off the sofa and walked softly to the light switch, but Jenny was awake before I reached it.

Luke, what's the time? Her voice was thickened by sleep and didn't sound like her own.

I don't know.

Is it too late to go out?

I switched the light on and squinted at my watch. No. It's just half past eight. Must have clouded over.

My arm's gone dead. Can you come and take Michael off it?

I glanced over at Christine as I moved back to the sofa. Her eyes were half open, hooded against the light. She was watching Jenny. I took Michael and rocked him while he grizzled awake. He must be starving, I said.

I know. Poor thing. She flexed her arm back and forth a few times. I know, she said again, this time to Michael who was already starting to bawl. I know, I know, she soothed. Just wait a second. You'll get your bottle in a minute. Mammy's a lazy cow and she's just waking up. She knows you're hungry.

Will he be okay to leave with Mrs Clement?

He'll be fine once he's fed. If he isn't, you and Chris go anyway.

I waited for Christine to say something but she just sat still, not even changing the posture she'd slept in. No, I said. If he plays up we'll stay in together. There's always tomorrow night.

Well, said Jen.

Look, I said. He's getting quieter already.

Let him suck your finger. I'll sort out the bottle.

While Jenny went up to the kitchen to prepare the milk, Christine stretched her whole body, catlike, in the armchair. She sighed as she relaxed again, then stood up and smoothed her denim skirt.

Look, I said to Michael. Here's Auntie Chris coming to say hello.

She smiled crookedly, as if to decline, but then came over to us anyway.

As soon as he realised she was near, Michael's attention was fixed. I drew my fingertip from his mouth.

Hello, little man, she said quietly. She touched his cheek with the backs of her fingernails and over her bent head I saw Jenny come back in from the corridor, shaking the bottle, still sleepy. Are you hungry? Christine murmured. Are you? Her head was close to my face now, her hair brushing my cheek as softly as she brushed his with her nails. As she spoke she slipped the tip of her index finger between his lips and at once his mouth closed tight and accepted it. Are you hungry? she whispered, and as he sucked hard, eyes fixed wide on her, she answered yes you are; yes you are.

The bottle's ready now, Jenny said a little sharply, moving toward us.

Christine stepped away, wiping her finger on his bib. She didn't look up as Jenny approached.

I'll take him, Jenny told me, standing in front of the sofa now, ready to sit with the bottle. Set him in my lap.

It was gone nine when we finally left Bethesda, and

Mrs Clement looked startled to be asked to babysit so late. Babies seemed to be one of the very few things she took any pleasure in, though, so it wasn't hard for Jenny to win her round with the promise that we'd be back before eleven. We were taking Christine to a choral concert at the campus Arts Centre, she lied, knowing from experience that both the Clements disapproved of drink. The night air was chilly and a high tide was slapping against the promenade wall, but both Jenny and Christine seemed glad to be out. They set off ahead of me up the crescent of the bay, linking arms as they walked.

Most of the seafront bars were quiet. Small huddles of students who'd lingered on through the long holiday or drifted back already for the autumn term sat at some of the bay-window tables and stared moodily out at us as we passed. I overheard Jenny apologising for the terrible nightlife and Christine laughed – going out drinking anywhere was a novelty, she said, so she had nothing much to compare it to.

Eventually they both turned to face me. I stopped in front of them and Jenny disengaged her arm from Christine's to take hold of both my hands. Where do you want to go? she asked. She swung my arms apart, then brought my hands together again, clasped in hers. I drew them back, embarrassed, and she let her own fall back to her sides. I shrugged.

Well, we could try the Cellar Bar, she suggested. That's pretty close by at least.

We haven't been there for years.

No, she agreed. Not since we were courting.

Courting, Christine laughed. That sounds so old-fashioned.

We *are* old-fashioned, Jenny insisted. Aren't we? she said, nudging her shoulders into my chest.

Looking ahead along the pavement I could see the blue lamps marking the steps down to the cellar, about fifty yards on. A light mist had come in with the tide and the lamps, along with the orange streetlights stretching down the prom, were haloed by it and seemed to be floating in mid-air.

We used to drink there a lot, she said, talking to Christine now. It was where we always used to meet. None of my other friends went there, so we could hide ourselves away.

I nodded, feeling awkward now. I could sense Christine's eyes on me, searching my face.

Come on, Jenny urged, and linked arms with us both until we reached the hazy blue lamps and the steps down to the bar.

A wooden signboard advertising a vodka promotion lay flat on its back at the foot of the steps. It was scuffed in the middle where someone had booted it down from the pavement.

Do you like vodka? Jenny asked Christine.

I don't know, she said. I've never drunk it.

Jenny laughed delightedly. You're joking! she said. My own sister, and she's never had vodka! What kind of life is that?

A couple of students appeared above us at the top of the steps. I pulled Jenny aside to let them get past then caught the door and held it open as it swung back after them.

Thanks, Christine said, and led the way in.

Not much had changed since we'd last been there – it

was still loud with piped rock music, dark, low-ceilinged and smoky. The wall lights were the only things that had altered. They still struggled to light anything past their own fittings but they were ultra-violet now and anyone wearing white in the bar was glowing faintly with a blueish phosphorescence. Maybe it was meant to liven the atmosphere up and suggest a nightclub ambience, but it gave the place a kind of sunken, submarine quality.

What do you want? I asked them both.

Jenny frowned and cupped her ear so I shouted the question again.

Get us a vodka and lime each, she barked back into the side of my head. With ice.

I pushed through to the bar, leaving Jenny yelling something to Christine about the lighting. Clapton's *Layla* suddenly started up through the speakers around the walls and a knot of drinkers blocking my way to the bar started jerking and swaying in time to the riff. One of them was Alex, the student teacher from the room next door. He'd obviously been drinking for quite a while. His hair was plastered to his forehead and his eyes were glassy-looking. He hadn't seen me so I ducked away from him and worked my way through another cluster of bodies to the far end of the bar.

Jenny and Christine had managed to find a table in one of the recesses along the back wall. There were four abandoned highball glasses already on it, three of them still half-full. Jenny took both vodkas from me and handed one to her sister. I perched myself on a stool alongside Jenny and sipped at my lager.

Well, what do you think? Jenny asked Christine.

Christine shrugged and tilted the drink to her lips for a

second taste. The light from the wall lamp above us made the vodka glow for an instant as it moved in the glass. I saw her throat relax and a measure of the fluid slipping down. Then she set the glass on the table and swirled the drink quickly, skipping the ice along the walls of the glass. It just tastes of lime juice, she said. I can't taste anything else at all.

Jenny laughed. You're not supposed to taste it; that's why it's great. I haven't had it since I fell pregnant, but I always drank vodka when I was a girl. Everyone did.

Christine shrugged again, though she seemed to consider this for a while. Well, I wouldn't know, she said. Then, do you remember Rosehip syrup? she asked.

Jenny looked puzzled.

When we were little, Christine prompted, staring at her now. It was pale red, and sweet. It sort of tasted like roses.

Recognition lit up Jenny's face and she nodded, smiling. Yes! she said. When we were really little. It smelt like perfume. We used to fight over it because we only got it if we were sick. And you always lied and said you were sick too if I was poorly and allowed to have some. She started laughing again. Mam kept it in the medicine cupboard, didn't she? I remember it perfectly now. Isn't that stupid? I hadn't thought about that for twenty years, but I can see her opening the cupboard and lifting it down for me.

Christine nodded, but she seemed lost in her own thoughts suddenly, just the ghost of a smile on her lips.

I can just picture it, Jenny went on, in amongst the brown cough medicine bottles. I used to think it was such a lovely colour, in the middle of them all. And that smell. Didn't we love the smell?

Christine took a long drink from her glass, letting one

of the ice cubes pass through and then sucking it hard while her sister spoke.

Where would you get that now? Jenny asked us both. Could you still get it? We should get some for Michael. She sipped her drink. Do you think they still make it? Maybe it's bad for a baby's teeth though. It must have been liquid sugar, it was so sweet.

I saw it in a chemist's window once, Christine said. She crunched on the ice cube and swallowed the shards. I nearly bought it for myself. I wanted to, she said.

Jenny laughed again, but Christine seemed to have grown sad, or distant, and soon we were all drinking wordlessly again.

I saw Alex at the bar, I told Jenny. He didn't see me.

The boy next door?

I nodded.

You didn't say hello?

He was pissed.

You could have said hello. She turned to Christine. He helps me out with Michael sometimes. If I need a baby-sitter for a little while when Luke's at work. He's really good like that. She turned back to me. You should have said hello, she insisted, disappointed with me. If I see him I'll say hello, she said. I might even ask him over. I'm going to the loo and then I'll get another round.

Christ, steady on, I said. I'm still fine with this.

We haven't got much time. Drink up, she ordered Christine. You need to make up for your boring teens.

Why do you call him the boy next door? Christine asked as soon as Jenny slipped away.

I shrugged. Because he lives next door.

She smiled. He's a fool, isn't he?

I must have looked surprised because she laughed at me, delighted. I met him, she said. With Jenny. We were in the kitchen. He took us down to his room and made a pot of herbal tea. She leered at me.

Why is he a fool?

She laughed again, as if the question was a huge joke. But she was right: secretly, and for no good reason at all, I despised him. I'd never thought much about it, but something in his harmless, easy-going friendliness made me angry and contemptuous. It was petty jealousy, I suppose. I understood instinctively, the first time I met him, that he belonged completely and sincerely in the world, in his skin, in his rickety Victorian room at Bethesda. It would have been impossible for him to live anywhere and not belong. He made me feel I was back at school or in the colliery again, resentful in the presence of so many comfortable Martians who breathed my own air better than me, and left me gasping. He was stronger than me, and everything that floated in from the world to the tiny pocket of place and time we randomly shared must, I felt at some deep level, belong to him.

I opened my mouth to speak again but Christine shook her head. Don't, she said simply, then reached out and took a long gulp from one of the highball glasses that had been left on the table. It was dark and flat – some kind of Coke mix. Ugh, she said and set it deftly back in the same spot she'd taken it from. So when is this party you're taking me to?

It took me a moment to understand what she meant. My mind was still on Alex and the way Christine had cut so effortlessly, so casually, to the truth. I knew Jenny would never have suspected the meanness of my contempt; not in a hundred years. *Yes, Jenny's a different species too,* I half-expected Christine to say. *And Michael too. They don't belong with you. You must hand them back.* I was almost waiting for it, and it terrified me.

Well? she said, and I realised I'd been lost in thought.

You mean Bill Kerrigan's party?

She nodded. I've been looking forward to it, she said, and her mouth pursed a little in the same way it just had when she'd tasted the flat, sweet drink in front of her.

Wednesday night.

She ran the tip of her tongue along her lips. She seemed distracted again suddenly. Then she smiled, focusing on me again. Kerrigan, she said. He's a fool too, isn't he? And despite the bright smile there was something intense in the way she said it, as if there was something suggestive in the idea.

No, he's fine, I protested. He's a nice guy.

Jenny called him a prick. When we were talking after you'd met him that time. Why does she think that?

I shrugged, uncomfortable. As far as I knew, Jenny still felt nothing more complicated than affection for Bill. I don't know. He's let us down a few times, promising things and then forgetting, you know? And I think Jenny and him were closer once, before I came on the scene. But he's never done anything bad to either of us. He's fine, I said again. I was confused at the way the conversation was going, and could feel my face becoming warm.

A prick, she repeated. Why is he a prick? Her lips parted a fraction, showing a glimpse of white.

I laughed and shrugged, trying to shake off a pressure I could feel building inside me. I needed air. I don't know. I don't think he is.

Her lips pursed back together, but tighter this time. Don't just tease, she said, and folded her arms loosely across her stomach.

A drunk girl flopped into the seat next to Christine, talking to a friend who remained standing at her side. Christine leaned over and spoke into her ear. The girl listened, stared at Christine a short while, then tugged at the friend's arm, stood up a little unsteadily, and left for another part of the bar.

I need the Gents, I said. I'll be back in a minute. I knew there'd be an open window there, and cool wet air blowing in from the sea.

Jenny and Christine were both at the table staring at fresh drinks when I was finally ready to go back through. The other glasses were all more or less empty and I knew Christine had swilled them down as soon as my back was turned, though why I couldn't guess. She ignored me when I sat down but Jenny leaned over and told me she'd talked to Alex and I was right, he was in a bad way.

I nodded just to show I'd heard her over the music and babble, then motioned for her to lean a little closer so I could put my mouth to her ear. Is everything alright? I asked. I mean with Christine.

Jenny pulled a face and shrugged subtly.

Is she upset?

Another tiny shrug. It's okay, I think. I don't know. Maybe she's just tired. Or maybe the vodka's going to her head. She's not used to it, is she?

I sat back and started on the fresh pint Jenny had bought for me, not needing it. Every so often Christine and Jenny exchanged words but mainly just drank steadily in short, compulsive sips. I nursed my pint through several of their rounds. At one point Jenny yelled to her over the music, with forced cheerfulness: has it hit you yet? Are you feeling the magic?

Christine smiled into space, then got up wordlessly and left the table to make for the bar again. It was getting crowded now and a local band had started setting up their gear in a far corner.

Jenny frowned, watching her go, then shifted her seat closer. She keeps staring around, Jenny shouted over the din. I think she's out of it. Should we take her home?

Yes, I shouted back. This is terrible.

I know. Sorry. It was a bad idea coming here. She moved her stool back then took another sip of whatever vodka mix she'd bought for the last round. She looked at me, swallowed and exaggerated a deep sigh.

Christine seemed a long time coming back with the drinks, and when she did she handed them to us wearing the same vacant expression that she'd left with.

Are you feeling ok? I yelled over the music as she set the glass down in front of me, spilling a little.

She turned a puzzled glance on me, then sat down and stared at the strangers milling about the table and moving to the music. They're like clumps of seaweed, swaying around underwater, she announced loudly.

I looked at Jenny and she raised her eyebrows. Drink up, she mouthed at me, and I nodded.

We shouldn't be too much longer, I heard her bark at Christine. We'd better not be late for Michael. She drained off the whole of her new drink in one and set the empty glass down firmly in front of her.

Christine peered down at her watch, studying it for a

few moments before dropping her arm to her side again. We could have one more, and then go, she said.

I could feel Jenny's frown bearing down on me from across the table, but it was my round so I avoided catching her eye. I think Jenny and me are fine, I said. I'll get you another one if you want though.

Have a vodka and lime with me – keep me company, she said, struggling to make herself heard and slurring quite badly now.

We can have a drink when we get back, Jenny interrupted. We've got more elderflower wine.

Christine grimaced. Go on, she pressed, ignoring Jenny. Have one with me. She almost touched my arm, but drew back and stirred a fingertip in the spilled beer instead.

Well, ok. But I'll have a whisky, not vodka, I said, still avoiding Jenny's glare.

Have something, Jennifer, she shouted at her sister, but Jenny shook her head, eyes fixed angrily on me.

Alex was still around and this time he caught my eye as I stood waiting at the taps. He wormed his way through to me and I noticed three young girls had tagged along behind him.

Luke, he said. He was beaming and made a great show of shaking my hand. Hey, I saw Jenny, he said. I wanted to bring you all a drink but I couldn't find you. He looked around him as if noticing for the first time that the place had become crowded.

The girls behind him were staring at me the whole time he spoke. They looked in as bad a state as Alex. Mr Lewis, who's your friend? one of them asked him.

This is Luke, he said over their heads, and belched. He

lives next door to me.

Hello, the one who'd spoken to Alex said. She was olive-skinned and slim, a little older looking than the other two though it was hard to tell exactly – they were all heavily made up. Even so, none of the three looked old enough to be drinking.

Let me get you a pint, man, now that I've found you, Alex broke in. I'll be right back. He lifted his hand to me and made for the toilets.

There was an awkward pause broken by the barman asking what I wanted. I ordered the vodka and whisky, hoping I could make my escape before Alex returned.

We're all in Mr Lewis' Social Studies class, the slim girl said while I waited for the drinks. We couldn't believe it when we saw him here. Do you know him really well?

Does he come here often? one of the other girls asked – a blond, plump kid with a pretty face.

Don't know. I'm never here. I looked at them more closely. Only the Mediterranean-looking kid seemed much over fifteen.

We come here quite a lot, she said, and the other two nodded solemnly. Mainly for the music. We know some of the guys in the bands.

I didn't have anything to say, so I nodded, wishing the barman would hurry up and get the drinks in front of me.

We couldn't believe it when we saw Mr Lewis, she went on. It's good when teachers go out, like normal people, isn't it?

Mr Lewis is great, the blond kid added. Is his first name Alex?

The drinks arrived and I reached to take the glasses.

Where's Mr Lewis? the third girl suddenly asked. She

was further gone than the other two. Her short-cropped hair was black, but her skin looked almost albino pale under the ultraviolet lights and the heavy make-up around her eyes made her seem mesmerised. I headed back for the table, leaving them staring patiently at the door of the Gents.

I was relieved to see Jenny and Christine talking again when I got to them, though the conversation died as soon as I took my seat. Christine drank quickly and Jenny didn't waste any time once she saw the glass was empty.

Ok then? she asked us both loudly.

Christine stood up obediently, then started looking about her feet. Did I bring anything? she asked.

Jenny shot me a glance. No, she shouted back, louder than she needed to.

I thought I did. She glared intently for a while at the legs of my seat. I feel like I did.

Come on, Jenny urged, looking at me.

I got up and Christine took hold of my arm, gripping it hard above the elbow. Ok? I asked her, surprised at the contact.

I'm fine. But help me get past all these chair legs.

I pushed the table away from her and shunted the stools clear with my foot. Her grip relaxed a little but she still kept hold until I'd walked her to the door, Jenny following along behind.

Outside, once we'd got up the narrow steps onto the pavement, Christine linked arms with me and rested her head against my shoulder as we walked. The night seemed to have grown warmer, though still humid, and the mist had vanished. Now the air had a soft, loaded feel to it and I could feel sweat beginning to prickle under the clamp of

Christine's arm and under the weight of her head. Near Bethesda, Jenny took hold of my hand on my free side and her palm was hot and moist. She squeezed my fingers hard and I turned my head to look at her. Don't worry, she whispered.

No, I'm not, I murmured back, not sure what she meant.

Michael had grizzled for an hour, then slept sound, Mrs Clements told us when we collected him at the door of their flat. He slept sweet as a little mouse, she said. Sweet as a mouse.

Thanks so much for having him, Jenny said quietly, smoothing Michael's wispy hair with the backs of her fingers as he started to grumble awake.

Well. And did you enjoy the concert? She eyed us sharply, obviously scenting drink. We'd sent Christine on up the stairs ahead of us, and I heard the muffled slam of one of the upstairs fire doors shutting behind her.

We had a lovely time, Jenny answered, already turning self-consciously and making as if to go.

Oh well. There's nice then, isn't it?

We'd best get him to bed before he comes round. Thanks again.

She watched us up the stairs to the first landing. Soon be in bed, Jenny crooned over Michael as we climbed the stairs. Soon be safe in bed.

Christine was waiting for us outside the apartment, leaning with her eyes shut against the doorframe. I wondered if she was sleeping on her feet, but when we got alongside she moved in on Jenny and Michael, stooping over his face to see him. I got the door open and Jenny went straight to the cot. I could tell she wanted him away from Christine, and I wondered if Christine felt it through all the drink.

Will you make coffee, Chris? Jenny asked when her sister appeared at her shoulder.

Love to, she said, brightly enough, but I thought I could see a stiffness in her face as she straightened up and drew away from the cot.

Michael cried while we were finishing our coffees, and it was late when we finally settled him again and got to bed. I used the bathroom last and on the way back down something made a sound, or caught my eye, and I stopped at the kitchen doorway to check inside. There was a figure standing in the dark, leaning back against the sink.

Who's there? I said, stepping back into the light.

Hey Luke, the figure drawled, and I realised it was Alex. I flicked the light switch and he winced.

I was getting some water. He raised a big red coffee mug to show me.

Don't throw up in here, I warned him.

No, man. No no.

A good night then?

He grinned slackly. Yeah. A good one. He took a big slug of water and grimaced as it went down.

Jenny was still sat up in bed when I got back. The main light was off but she had the tiny lamp that popped up out of her radio alarm clock still on, angled onto the side of her face. She was reading a magazine but folded it closed as soon as I came through the door. She watched me undress, then followed me with her eyes as I rounded the bed and climbed in beside her.

Has everything been all right today? she asked as soon

as I was settled. I'm sorry we went out tonight – it spoiled things, didn't it?

I shrugged. It was ok, I said. It was good for us to get out, maybe. A bit of a break from looking after Michael.

Jenny looked away, worrying at a nail with her teeth. Chris was strange, though, she said eventually. She went quiet on the beach, and then stayed moody all the time after that.

I kept quiet. I hadn't heard Jenny criticising Christine at all during her visit before then, and suddenly I got the feeling there was something starting to push under the smiles. I was unnerved, and curious, feeling the change in Christine too, but just shrugged again. I didn't want her to go on.

Well. Maybe it's just me, Jenny said.

I don't know. I think everything's ok.

She must have drawn blood then because she winced and sucked at the corner of the nail. I don't know, she said. It was like the old Chris was maybe coming back again.

Down on the seafront a car skidded, revved madly and roared off again along the prom. Anyway, Jenny went on, inspecting the nail she'd torn, I'm going to take a few more days off work. Do you think that's a good idea?

I had a couple of long afternoon spells at the warehouse fixed for the week ahead, and at first we'd planned to let Christine look after Michael while we were both out. I understood what Jenny was hinting at now though – she didn't want Christine alone with Michael anymore.

It'll mean you don't have to entertain her all on your own, she said. It wouldn't be easy for you if she had another moody day like today. And I can take care of Michael so Chris can go out and not get bored. What do you think?

I'm easy, I said, wondering what I actually felt, but not able to name it. I realised I was scratching where the sores had been, raking up the small scabs around my middle. I stopped and let the skin burn.

It means I won't have any more holidays left, but this is our holiday in a way – having Christine to stay and taking her out to places like the beach and the pub. We wouldn't do that normally any more, would we? Not with Michael.

No.

She was quiet for a minute or so, then reached across and snapped the little alarm clock lamp down. She curled herself into a foetal position and wedged her pillow more comfortably under her head. I'm so sleepy, she mumbled. It's been a long day. She yawned and shifted the pillow again. I can't believe we were on the cliffs this morning. Then she was still.

I stayed sitting up, staring into the dark, digging at the skin again where it was flaming.

That dog was terrible, wasn't it? Her voice was drowsy and distant now, muffled by the pillow. I thought it was going to bite Michael. I really did. That stupid man. I wanted to kill him.

I could hear her breathing when she wasn't speaking. It seemed to come straight from the back of her throat, like every breath was a sigh.

Jen, I said.

What?

I was talking to Christine in the church. Is it right that he used to take you all around the country visiting churches when you were small? I mean when you were all together, as a family.

She thought about it for a moment, then snorted. No.

That's nonsense. Why on earth would she tell you that?

I knew I had to carry on then. She told me something else, too. She said your father committed suicide. When she was looking after him, after the last heart attack.

For a few seconds the breathing went on the same as before. Then there was silence.

Did you know? I went on. Is it true?

She lay still for quite a while, and I stayed sitting upright, staring at the red digital numbers on her clock radio. I watched the colon between the hours and minutes blinking with every second. I felt dizzy, and vaguely frightened.

I don't know, she said at last. But she had no right to talk to you about it, without me there. And you had no right to let her. She blamed me, didn't she?

I put my hand out and stroked her shoulder but she tensed and kept her back to me.

Don't bother answering, she said flatly, still speaking into her pillow. I know she did. I know. Oh Christ. She made a strange sound in the back of her throat and I realised she was biting back sobs. I can't believe you're doing this to me, she said, recovering her breath. You remind me of him sometimes, she said heavily. The way he was before he turned so religious and strange. I read once that it can happen like that. You can keep falling for your father, even when you hated him. Maybe especially when you hated him. She took a deep breath and choked another sob back. And you remind me of her.

I don't know how long we lay there then, not moving, hardly breathing, even. I had no idea what she meant, and was lost in thought, puzzling over it, for what seemed like a long, black time. But then there was a noise from

Christine's room, just a faint judder as something, maybe
a naked foot, moved on the floorboards, and immediately
I was aware of everything around me again, and was
straining to listen. A faint line of light showed under the
door. She was still awake, maybe reading; or listening,
like me. Jenny was shivering, I realised, though to me the
air was uncomfortably warm. I shifted closer, edging my
skin against hers. There was another sound from behind
Christine's door, a softer, scraping noise this time. Maybe
she'd pulled something – a book maybe – over the floor
towards her, or pushed it away.

Jenny, I said softly.

What?

I moved my hand down along her arm, onto her hip-
bone, prominent and smooth, then around and between
her thighs. She turned her head towards me a fraction so
I leaned closer and kissed her cheek, her neck, the lobe of
her ear.

Luke, she said sadly, but I didn't know what she meant
by it.

I must have slept at some point because the next thing I
remember is waking to the sound of the apartment door
clicking open and shut. I was still flat on my back on top of
the covers but Jenny was beside me now, curled under the
sheets, her back to me. At first I wondered if I'd dreamed
the sound but when I raised my head to check Christine's
door I could see it was just ajar. Maybe she'd opened it in
the night as we slept, or maybe the draught from the main
door had nudged it off the catch. I let my head drop to the
pillow again and waited for the sound of her returning.
I wondered if Jenny was awake too. Her breathing was

shallow, which made me unsure, but it was steady and slow enough. Upstairs the flush hissed faintly and I angled my face towards the main door again, waiting to watch her stepping through it.

It was well in to the morning when I woke. Behind the door – closed tight again now – I could hear Jenny's muffled voice, then Christine's. I got out of bed, dressed quickly and went through to join them. They were both dressed and standing at the window, Michael in Jen's arms. The window was open and through it I could smell the sea and hear the steady chop of helicopter blades. Because of the noise neither of them noticed me behind them until I was almost at their shoulders, then Jenny caught sight of me and moved aside without saying anything.

About half a mile out from the beach a yellow rescue helicopter was thumping over the water. It hovered for a while then swung out slowly toward the headland. I imagined Christine swimming out there just a few hours before: the speck of her head making its way almost invisibly amongst the dark crests and swells.

I'm going to the shop, Christine said. Do you want me to get anything in particular?

No, said Jenny. Just bread and milk.

She left us to find her purse, then headed out without a word.

Do you want breakfast? Jenny said eventually.

No. I'll just get a coffee.

A young seagull, almost full-grown but still in its grey herringbone plumage flapped onto the sill. I moved to close the sash window and it launched itself back into the air with a scream.

Christ, it almost flew right in, Jenny said, startled.

I glanced down at Michael to see if he'd noticed, but his eyes were shut fast.

The helicopter reached the headland, then swung back across the mouth of the bay. It was farther out now, and the sound of it was much fainter.

The phone in the corridor started ringing. I'll get it, I said.

Hey, Luke, Anzani said when I answered it. I need a favour, ok? I need someone to drive my van for a day or two. How would you like that? Just a few days. It's better money than the warehouse. You know how to drive, Luke, eh?

I told him I did, but didn't tell him that the last time I'd driven anything other than the tractor on Pugh's farm was when I took my driving test almost three years before.

It's just deliveries. A few afternoons. My boy can cover some of the time, but not all, you know? My real driver, Mike, he's off in the hospital for a couple of days.

Ok, I said, that should be fine.

Good. I'll need you tomorrow at three.

When I went back through and told Jenny the arrangement she said she thought it was all right. Now that she was taking more holidays it wouldn't be so awkward with Michael. It means he'll have to come with us if Christine and me go anywhere, but that's ok, she said. She knew we had a baby when she decided to come.

Well. I don't think she'd mind anyway.

Jenny didn't answer. I could tell she was still angry, or hurt, from what I'd told her the night before, but I could think of nothing I could do or say about that. I wondered if she might confront Christine at some point. Clearly she hadn't yet.

I'll make coffee, I said, and with that Christine opened the door and brought the shopping in.

Chris, we'll have to change some of our plans for the week, Jenny said flatly.

Why? What's wrong, her sister replied, but without a trace of disappointment or surprise.

Luke has to work some afternoons now. Anzani phoned when you were out and asked him to drive the delivery van this week, so he won't be able to look after Michael.

It's not a problem, Christine breezed.

I stared at her. I don't think I'd ever seen her so relaxed and carefree-looking. She seemed a completely different person to the inscrutable drunk of the night before.

Where do you have to go in the van? she asked, facing me with a bright, open smile.

I don't know. From what he said, mainly in town, but he sells wholesale to quite a few places so he'll probably have me going out to some of the villages, too.

Well, I could help Luke some days, she said to Jenny, looking her in the eye. I could be his navigator. I'd like to see some of the little places out of town. Would you mind that? She turned to me again, so that it wasn't clear which of us she'd addressed the question to.

That's fine by me, I said.

Is that all right? she asked Jenny directly then. Do you mind?

Jenny turned away, back to the window and the sea. There was no sign of the helicopter now. She squeezed Michael and rocked him gently. No, she said. Why would I mind?

Six

It seems strange and defeating to me, the older I've become and the more I've seen, that while the life of the mind can be so mysterious and subtle, the life of the body is as comic and crude and predictable as graffiti. The one life carries the other into all kinds of slapstick and disasters, over and over again; and the body's is the stronger life, and does the carrying, whatever else we like to pretend. And for everyone other than fanatics or saints, there seems to be no other way to love.

My father left my mother the morning she caught him hunched and grunting over the brassy blond manageress of a caravan park in Porthcawl. We'd gone there as usual for our yearly holiday and he'd been late coming back from her office, where he'd said he was going to complain about a leak in the Gents toilet block. They were using her desk, my mother told me later that night, babbling more to herself than to me in a stunned, mechanical attempt to make sense of this thing that she'd stepped onto like a landmine.

I don't know if my mother would have forgiven him in time, or at least grown to tolerate the memory, because he never gave her the chance. He declared his love for the woman – a youngish widower called Mrs Hooper who'd been left the fairly lucrative business – and refused point blank to take us home. Instead, he paid for the big black taxi that ferried my mother and me away, exhausted and dazed after a night of tears and rain that I still can't bring to mind without feeling physically ill.

When I was nine, a couple of years after this, he took it into his head that I should visit for a weekend in the summer holidays, more from a sense of entitlement than any serious desire to spend time with me I think, and against my mother's raging and pleading I agreed. The chance of gaining any kind of recognition from him overrode every other instinct and pressure.

There was no chance of it reconnecting us, of course. He'd diversified the business by buying up a pub just down the road from the caravan park – The Oak – and I spent most of the weekend in the beer garden there, where a tall, spreading oak tree did in fact grow and shade the lunchtime drinkers. I whiled away the hours reading the American comic books that my step-brother owned and had been instructed to share with me. I'd had my own instructions from my father on arrival at the bus station: to 'make damn sure you make an effort with him, and don't take advantage just because he's not the full shilling, and get along nice.'

It wasn't difficult to obey. Jason, the woman's only child, was three years older than me in age but simple-minded and good natured. Left alone with him in the beer garden for the first time he told me that I could learn his name best by thinking of it as Jasun. Jasun-up-in-the-sky, he explained. We pored over well-thumbed copies of The Silver Surfer together – American comics were exotic to me, though I'd seen other boys at school reading and swapping them of course – and I read the more complex pieces of dialogue out loud for him, as utterly swept up by the grand, melancholy plots as Jason. At night I took them to bed with me and read them cover to cover again until I fell asleep, already in a dream of gliding in silence, silver skinned, nameless, history-less and utterly alone, through an ocean of rolling planets and stars, none of them home.

When the weekend was over I knew in my boy's heart that the experiment, for all my wild, desperate hopes, had failed. My father had been at an utter, shamefaced loss whenever he'd run out of excuses about the busyness of his work and simply had to make some kind of conversation with me. Maybe it was delayed guilt for that awful, endless night I'd spent unable to comfort my broken mother in the caravan, or for the pitiful cowardice he'd shown in ordering that taxi for us, or maybe it was plain, male boredom; either way, I know we both felt the strain of having to pretend that the visit might be repeated, knowing full well that it wouldn't.

Just before my mother's death my father abandoned his second family for the gold mines of Australia, and nobody from those days, as far as I know, has ever heard from him since.

Before Michael was born, and for months after, I used to wake in the early hours worrying, having had no kind of fatherly example to follow. And God knows I was right to be afraid. But I didn't imagine I could lose him so completely; lose him as if I'd let him vanish into space. Michael, Michael: my father's own name, who vanished to the other side of the world, into another continent's dusty ground. And Michael my only son. Where are you now? Where have you gone? Jason, we could have named him if I'd known. Another poor Jason-up-in-the-sky.

★

I remember Jenny waking me once, when Michael was nearly due and we hadn't long moved into our rooms at Bethesda. She was sat up in bed, shivering, but not making any noise except for her breath catching and giving. When she saw I was awake she stopped juddering and just sat hunched over in the bed, not answering when I asked her what was wrong.

In the end she said, I had such a vivid dream that you were dead. Lying beside me dead. All blue and cold.

By the time she'd brought herself to speak I could feel myself drifting back into sleep, so I made myself sit up alongside her.

Don't sit up, she said, but I stayed there anyway.

It was the first time in months that Jenny had been woken by a nightmare. When we first started living together it happened every couple of days or so, and if it wasn't that, it was talking wildly in her sleep, whole strange arguments and bargainings, even when she was supposed to be knocked out with pills. I dreaded it, but it had gradually got better, and because there was nothing that seemed to disturb the surface of her waking life I quickly forgot each episode in the routine of the daytimes that followed.

I couldn't get out of the dream, she said now, even though I knew I was dreaming, and when I woke up properly it was so quiet I really felt it was true. I was so afraid. I was too afraid to move and touch you. I didn't know what to do. Christ, she said, then started half laughing, half sobbing. She stopped quite quickly and straightened her back for a big, clearing sigh. I'm wide awake now, she said. I'm so thirsty.

I'll get some water, I said. It was a warm, airless night and my mouth was parched too.

Don't put the light on, she said.

Are you sure?

Yes. Don't, please.

I touched her arm to reassure her, then climbed out of bed.

Make tea, she called softly as I got to the bedroom door.

I boiled the kettle in the living room and made two mugs of weak tea. I carried them back through into the bedroom, leaving the door open behind me so enough light would get in to show me what I was doing.

We sat up another hour or so and Jenny ended up talking about her father, and how her mother, every morning for months after the split, made the two girls promise to tell her if he ever turned up at the school to try and see them, or if he ever gave them any cards or letters to read. I remember I was surprised and interested because it was something she hardly ever mentioned. She told me that after a while Christine rebelled and started going into hysterics every time she was questioned about him, and it seemed that he must have been seeing her somehow because when the appeal for custody came through she started the long, remorseless mutiny.

Did you want to go with him too? I asked.

Even in the gloom I could see her staring at me as if I were mad. No, she said. I knew by then he was a monster. I was old enough to understand.

I didn't ask what she meant, though now of course I wish I had. Maybe everything then would have turned out differently, all the rest of our lives. But I didn't, and I never did; I was too wary, or innocent, or lazy, and what happened to us happened. Maybe I resisted knowing because we'd both seen so much damage caused by love already in our parents' lives and more than anything I wanted our own lives to escape all that, to not get too close and become infected. I don't know, and didn't know then, but it was one of those lonely, unsignposted crossroads in the life of the mind. Maybe the old Blues singers were right, and the devil waits there for us, patient, under a big empty sky, kicking his heels in the dust. Instead I asked, why did Christine want to go with him?

She pinched her lower lip between her front teeth and shook her head. It was Christine he wanted. And she was younger. Maybe she didn't know any better. And we were terrible to each other, you know, the way sisters can be. Maybe she wanted to get away from me.

That was one of the very few times before her father's death that Jenny ever mentioned Christine. For a long time after I'd got to know her she was happy for me to think she was an only child – her mother too, on the few occasions I met her – and I remember sitting in bed that night wondering if she'd tell me anything more about this shadowy, wilful little stranger now that she'd got onto the subject, but it didn't happen. And as so often in the years to come, I failed to help bring anything into the light. She fell silent for a while and finished her tea.

I'm frightened about this, too, she said eventually, and let her hand drift over her stomach.

In the dark, an image of what was under her palm came into my mind – a tiny, stubborn, blind clot of tissue, feeding on the blood. I swilled back the last of my tea.

I'm scared I won't be allowed to keep it, like a punishment, she said. She avoided looking at me. Do you know what I mean? Do you ever feel that too?

A punishment for what? I said. That doesn't make sense. You can't think like that.

I know it's mad; that's sort of what I mean.

I didn't mean it like that. I didn't mean mad; I meant stupid. Pointless.

There was quiet between us for a while, and I wished I hadn't answered her at all. I'm sorry, I said at last. I didn't mean that you were stupid. I just meant that I didn't understand. I don't like it when you talk like that. I don't know what to say.

She reached out for a tissue from the bedside table and blew her nose. I'm just tired of losing things, she said. I'm sorry too. Let's go to sleep. I just wanted to tell you, that's all.

Seven

Before we leave to meet Jenny at the Half Moon I feed Michael and that helps to quieten him down, though he gets big, upset hiccoughs from the baby food and he only really settles when I start strapping him into the push-chair. It often works like that. Sometimes when he's really playing up we just strap him in and push him round the room, out into the corridor, up and down the scraggy carpet until he sleeps. He stares at my fingers now as I fasten the last buckles across his chest.

We pass Mrs Clement on the stairs. She's brushing them hard and collecting big tangles of hair in a red plastic dust-pan which is just about full. She's not often out of her window seat but sometimes takes it into her head to spruce a patch of carpet up. Maybe her nervous energy builds up day after day and sometimes gets the better of her. The regular cleaner calls once a week but doesn't touch the rooms or kitchens. We're all long-stay tenants here and supposed to keep our own nests clean.

She doesn't like us taking Michael downstairs in his chair, and she eyes me up now as I lower him onto the step she's brushing.

You'll kill that baby one day, she says confidently.

I can't think of any good answer, so I just wait till she moves her gear and lets me past.

Is he all strapped in? She plucks at his chest-bands as I bump him gently to the next stair.

I nod and she gives up, taking her hands off him and brushes a few strands of pewter-grey hair from her face with the back of one of the bright pink rubber gloves she's wearing. The rest of her hair is pinned up in a tight, gleaming bun. She never cuts it, she told Jenny once. A woman's hair is her glory, she told her, and quoted the biblical reference for it, chapter and verse.

Once I'm past her big haunches I speed up a little. Michael's sitting very calm, like a racing driver in his wool helmet and gloves.

You'll kill him, you will, she calls after me.

Righto, I call back.

All the way along the prom I find myself scanning the backs or faces of women across the street or making their way up the prom ahead of us. Twice I run Michael's chair blindly over a kerb, jolting him. The second time he bites his tongue but it's only when a passer-by, a young girl, tells me he's bleeding that I realise it. I thank the girl and stoop down to see to him. The kid hangs around even after I say, don't worry, he's fine, I'll see to it. In the end I have to tell her she's making him nervous so she'd better go, and then she turns slowly before carrying on down the street.

Michael's chin is a mess, his spittle frothing up the blood and bubbling it all the way down to his neck. I use a handkerchief to get the worst off, and once I've cleaned him up it's obvious there's not much real bleeding it was just his swollen tongue making him drool it all.

When we get to The Half Moon I wheel the chair round the side entrance and into the beer garden. It's deserted and the parasols over the tables are folded and tied despite the sunshine. For a moment I wonder if the garden is out of use for some reason, but then I notice a pair of empty pint glasses on a corner table. I wheel Michael over to the corner, collect the glasses and go indoors to the bar. A few customers are sat quietly on the high stools in front of the taps watching the news on a TV at the end of the bar. The barman's watching it too, and I have to clear my throat to get his attention.

Back in the garden, Jenny arrives ten minutes late looking rushed and unsettled. She gives me a weak smile and sits opposite us both, taking a drink from the half pint of cider I had waiting for her. I'll have to get back sooner than I thought, she apologises. It got busy after I called. Sorry.

That's ok, I tell her.

I picked up some rolls on the way, she says. It'll be quicker than ordering something. They take forever to do any food here. She takes them from her shoulder bag and we eat them quickly with our drinks.

What's wrong with Michael? She puts her glass on the table and crouches in front of him.

I can feel my colour rise. I take a swig of beer.

Christ, there's blood in his mouth. Luke!

He bit his tongue coming up the prom, don't worry. I cleaned him up – he's fine.

She opens his mouth wider with her fingers and he tries to twist his face away. He's fine, I tell her again. It's nothing. He's not even grizzling.

When she's satisfied she gets up and adjusts his bonnet, then comes and sits beside me on the wooden bench. She's even more edgy now. I thought he'd hurt himself, she says. I thought he'd found some glass and eaten it – there must be lots of bits of glass somewhere like this. We shouldn't have brought him here. She takes a deep breath and puffs it out.

What's wrong? I say.

She shakes her head. I'm ok. I just got a bit of a scare. Neither of us wants to make eye contact but she rests a hand on my leg. I didn't mean to make a fuss, she says. She looks like she's poised to say something more, but it doesn't come. Instead a young barmaid steps out into the yard and makes for our table.

I'll put this up, she says, and leans over the bench to open up the parasol.

A black cocoon made by some caterpillar plops into my beer from out of the folds, but the barmaid doesn't notice, or pretends not to. She hurries back into the bar and I fish out the little casing with a finger. I look at Jenny and for the first time in days she lets out a genuine laugh. I lay it down on the table and roll it gently back and forth with a fingertip, careful not to crack it.

I'll get you another drink, she says.

God no. I'm not bothered. I leave the cocoon alone and take another swig to prove it. Jenny laughs again, creasing her eyes in disgust at the same time, and I'm smiling with her now. I try to recall the last time I made her laugh out loud but can't seem to picture it at all. Then I realise my mind has shifted onto wondering whether Christine would be laughing at what's just happened and a cold, quenching hand reaches up inside and kills my smile. How was your morning, I say?

She grimaces and looks down at the table. Not so good, she says.

I realise she wants me to chase her a little, but I can't bring myself to. The girl who opened the parasol comes back out and rescues me. She stands at the table tapping her notebook with the rubber butt of her pencil.

We don't need food, Jenny tells her.

Oh. Ok, she says, then leaves us.

When I look back at Jenny it's obvious I'll find out what's wrong anyway – she's got her head bowed and the next move will have to be mine. What is it? I say.

No answer.

I look at Michael. He's staring around, content.

What? I say, trying to keep the rising panic I feel out of my voice.

She takes a slow breath. I'm just being stupid, she says. I'm ok.

Tell me.

I got a fright this morning, she says at last. She's put a hand on Michael's bonnet, twisting the wool ball on top, winding it tight one way, then the other.

What kind of fright?

It sounds stupid now.

Tell me.

Her fingers are still working on the bonnet. Michael's trying to reach up to find out what's going on up there, but she doesn't notice.

Well, she says, you know how my office window looks out onto the arcade?

I nod. The arcade – a crumbling, ratty passageway of boarded up booths and a public toilet – links the far end of the prom and the High Street where Jenny works. I start to guess what Jenny might have seen. Drunks beating each other half to death; maybe some old dosser, dead or dying, getting shovelled into an ambulance. Those kinds of things happened there now and again, and always upset her.

Well, she carries on, a girl came out with a pushchair and she was wearing a green jacket like Christine's. And I thought she'd taken Michael. She looks set to cry.

I force a laugh. Christ, Jen, I say.

I know, I know. She stops toying with Michael's bonnet and puts both hands in her lap. I thought oh God, he's let her take my baby, she blurts suddenly, and I feel my stomach roll.

We finish our drinks in silence and after a while I reach out to touch her hand where it's lying flat on the table.

These last few days, she says quietly, but doesn't finish.

You're just tired, I tell her. Just tired and not thinking straight.

She draws her hand away and rests it in her lap. It's getting colder again, she says, and it's true: when I left Bethesda the sky was a wide, soft blue, but now there's a mass of dark cloud riding in on a chilly breeze from the north.

I can smell rain, she says. Make sure Michael doesn't get caught in it, if it comes. There's something weary in the way she's speaking now; withdrawn, almost resigned. This morning in the office, she says, after seeing the woman with the baby, I was thinking how I've never really told you things. I haven't really trusted you, and I should have. I'm sorry now.

God, Jenny. What's that supposed to mean? You're going on like one of us was dying. I take a deep breath, panic stitching inside my guts like a needle. It's not important, I tell her, feeling my voice tighten up as I speak. It's up to you what you tell me. I don't tell you everything either.

She closes her eyes and doesn't reply, though I can see I've hurt her. We sit awkwardly for a while, then I check my watch. As I let my arm drop she says, why aren't you frightened of Christine?

Before I can ask her what she means someone calls her name from the doorway of the bar, a young blond guy with tight, curly hair and a confident, dimpling smile.

Who's that? I ask her.

Drew, she says quickly and quietly, then smiles up at him and waves. He's already heading toward us. I'm sorry, she says, just before he gets within earshot.

He stops just beyond arm's length. So this is where you disappeared to, he says.

She turns to face me. Luke, this is Drew, he works in the records department.

In the bowels, he says. We're in the basement, he explains brightly, turning to me for the first time.

He can't be older than eighteen. There's an easy, well-scrubbed chubbiness about his face that makes me want to punch it.

Is that your baby? he says, leering at Michael.

Michael looks back at him.

What time are you going back? Drew asks her.

She checks her watch. Ten minutes.

He sniffs and for a moment I think he's about to leave us alone, but no. I let the conversation roll over me, though the kid's voice grates on my nerves whenever he raises it to laugh or emphasise a point, which is often. I try to blank my mind of everything, and instead find myself remembering Jason and his comic books, in that other beer garden, on that vanished afternoon. Finally I reach out for the little black cocoon on the table in front of me and concentrate on rolling it between finger and thumb, building the pressure minutely, feeling for the critical point where the case would give way at the tiniest increase.

Well, I'd better be getting back. Drew looks at me and lifts his hand. Nice meeting you, he says.

I tell him it was nice to meet him too, and I can feel Jenny frowning at my tone of voice. The wind feels like it's getting colder by the minute. I can feel it tugging at my shirt sleeves.

She's quiet again once he's gone. Then she says, you don't need to be so hostile. You're always like that with people I know. You get growly, like a bad tempered dog.

It's partly true, so I don't argue. I don't want to argue about anything, anyway. I realise I'm still holding the cocoon. For some reason I don't want Jenny to see me putting it back on the table so I let it drop to the ground.

There's silence for a while, then she tells me she'll have to go soon, and I nod.

Sorry, I say.

No. I shouldn't have dragged you out. It doesn't matter. Look after Michael on the way back. It's got colder. Don't hang around with him in the wind, will you?

No.

And forget about what I said earlier. I was just a bit upset. I wish I hadn't phoned now.

Don't worry.

I'm not worried. I just wish I hadn't. She bends down and kisses Michael, checks the inside of his mouth one more time, then tightens the ribbons holding the bonnet under his chin. When it's secure enough she stands and slips her handbag over her shoulder. I'll be back late, she says. I've got to get through some of the work that built up last week. What a waste of time that all was, in the end.

I don't know what to say to that, so I take our empty

glasses and nest one inside the other.

I'll be home around seven.

Jen, I say. I take some air in and steady my voice. Why don't you take the afternoon off sick? You could take a couple of days. We could go away somewhere. Just for a few days. I don't know. Suddenly my chest feels like it's loaded with stones. It's hard to breathe right and I can hardly bear to look her in the eye.

She shakes her head. I took all the days I could for Christine. I can't take more time now. She takes a close, half-puzzled last look at me, like she's trying to remember who I am, then turns to go. Bye, she says, and then she's gone, and we're alone.

The sun keeps breaking through and disappearing again as I wheel the buggy back along the prom. A few cold spits of rain have started to speckle the pavement. A few hundred yards or so before Bethesda I notice Bill Kerrigan on the opposite side of the road, heading into town, hands deep in the pockets of his duffel coat. He's walking with quick, long strides, glancing every now and then out to sea. He doesn't give any sign of noticing me and soon we've passed each other by. On our side of the street a yellow council cleaning truck is whining ahead of us, crawling along and holding up the traffic, the big flared brushes on its underside spraying grit and storm-shingle off the tarmac and into the hubs and paintwork of parked cars. I speed up and hurry the buggy past it. Michael, sleepy now, half-opens his eyes as we draw alongside but doesn't seem bothered by the bedlam of engines and rotors flailing just a few feet away from his head.

As we draw closer I realise there's some kind of

gathering across from Bethesda. A small crowd of dark-dressed people, clustered at the railings overlooking the sea. Then I realise they're school-kids in uniform, young teenagers, some twenty or thirty of them, standing in a rough semi-circle. At the edge of the group a young woman keeps watch over them. She looks agitated, stalking back and forth at the edge of things, grimacing, though none of the kids are playing up.

A tall, straight-backed man in a charcoal suit and minister's collar, is addressing them, staring balefully over their heads at some fixed point beyond them which might be the bay window of Bethesda. I wonder if Mrs Clement is staring back at him. I can't make out what he's saying but then the kids start singing, self-consciously, uneasy maybe at the onlookers collecting around them. *We rest on thee,* they moan, *our shield and our defender.*

Halfway up the steps I see Clement lurking behind the glass panels of the front door. He opens it for me as I arrive at the top step, then nods sombrely as I steer Michael past him.

Well, Luke, he says meditatively, leaving the door open to stare more easily out at the singers. Look at this, he murmurs, and prods the steel bridge of his spectacles to bring the lenses closer to his grey eyes. Look now, he says again, and I stop despite myself and turn to watch with him. He shifts a little to let me get a clearer view and as he moves I catch a faint scent of stale sweat from his shirt. As the hymn draws to a close he starts to sing along, his voice soft and narcotic. *Victors we rest, with thee through endless days. Vic-tors-we-rest with thee through end-less days.* A local boy, see, he says. Swept away last week.

I nod, remembering the yellow helicopter sweeping

back and forth over the bay. I hadn't thought much about it at the time or afterwards – it wasn't too rare a sight, and might have been a training exercise for all anyone could know.

Man is as grass, see, Luke. As grass, he sighs. Well, well.

Across the road the minister goes through his benediction, lifting his arms, face turned to the sky. The kids all bow their heads, though the young teacher keeps a furtive watch. Then it's over and they're all herded back up the prom, some of the girls linking arms, looking like they might be sobbing, or gossiping. There's a white wreath tied to the rail where the minister was standing. The onlookers linger for a while, some of the more curious stooping to read the cards attached to the flowers. Then everyone drifts on and I'm left listening to Clement humming the tune of the hymn again.

I'd better get going, I tell him, I've got to drop off Michael with Mrs Clement and get to work. He stops mid-note and peers at me as if I've startled him awake.

Eight

The Monday evening passed slowly and quietly after Anzani's phone call. Jenny complained of being tired and seemed to shut herself off from all of us, even Michael, for long stretches of time. I read and watched TV on the sofa with Christine while Jenny, curled in the big armchair opposite us, leafed through some of the magazines she'd bought while they'd wandered the shops and cafes in the week before. At ten she suggested an early night. Christine agreed and that was just about the only communication they had all evening.

At breakfast on the Tuesday, when Christine had showered after her swim and was towelling her hair in front of the window, Jenny mentioned that maybe Anzani wouldn't be too happy about her riding with me in his van. He might think you're taking advantage, she said.

Advantage of what? Christine asked, watching me rather than her sister.

Jenny finished feeding Michael a blob of mush she'd scraped together from what was left of his rusks. It just might look odd, she said, if he sees you. He doesn't know who you are. You could be anyone. It might put Luke in an awkward position.

I shifted uncomfortably in my seat. I can pick Chris up after I collect the van, I said. He won't see her then.

For some reason neither of them seemed satisfied with that and the atmosphere stayed uneasy. Jenny shrugged and scratched together one last spoonful of rusk for Michael. He pursed his lips and tried to butt it away. Jenny let him be and dropped the full spoon back in his bowl. Is everyone done? she said. She looked at the empty plates and bowls on the table, then started stacking them briskly on top of her own.

Every other morning since she'd arrived Christine had cleared the breakfast things and brought back coffees from the upstairs kitchen. Now, taken by surprise, she folded her towel and stared at Jen. I can do that, she said.

There's no need.

I'd like to.

Well, so would I today. I don't like sitting around looking at dirty dishes.

Christine's cheeks coloured faintly. I would have done it, she said.

Jenny shrugged. I just feel like doing it now.

Okay. Thanks. Christine left the towel on a radiator and joined me on the sofa. I could smell apples in the shampoo she'd used.

You see to Michael, Jenny said quietly to me, as if speaking privately.

As soon as Jenny left for the kitchen, Christine got up from the sofa, found her trainers and tugged them onto her feet. I'm going for a walk, she said. What time are you going to get the van?

Not till the afternoon. About three.

Well. I might not be back for lunch. If I'm not, where should I meet you?

I could pick you up here.

No. Somewhere in town. She shifted her weight

restlessly from one foot to another and I could tell she wanted to get away before Jenny returned.

What places do you know?

She shrugged. The castle, museum, library... some pubs and shops. I know all the big shops so I could meet you outside any of them.

They'd be a pig to park a van in front of, when there's traffic. How about the library?

She was already edging to the door. Fine, right. At three?

Just after. About ten past.

The water pipes behind the wall groaned as someone ran hot water somewhere in the building. Probably Jenny in the kitchen. I'm your guest now, she said, calmly and definitely. You know that, don't you? She looked me in the eye and I had to turn away. I'm going then, she said. Bye. She left without closing the door, her hair still damp and limp.

I checked Michael's nappy, cleaned his face, then took him to the window and waited for Jen.

Where's Christine? she asked as soon as she stepped through the open door.

Out for a walk.

Oh. That's nice. I take extra days off work so she doesn't have to get bored and she disappears without me. That's really nice. She went through to the living room and folded herself into the armchair, legs drawn up under her.

She might not be long, I lied.

Jenny didn't bother answering. Bring Michael through, she called after a little while.

I took him to her. I'll make coffee, I said, handing him

down.

Thanks, she said, standing Michael on her thighs, propping him under his armpits. He swayed wide-eyed but disinterested. She jiggled him, wanting a response, and he dribbled. I put the kettle on to boil while I was up there, she said. I meant to bring the coffee down with me but I forgot when I heard somebody going down the stairs. Sorry. She leaned forward and let Michael down onto the floor.

There were three mugs set out ready in the kitchen. I put the kettle on and while it came back to the boil I rinsed the paste of coffee grains, milk and sugar out of Christine's cup. Back out on the stairs I passed the tall, middle-aged man I'd seen in the corridor with Clement the week before. He was wearing a shapeless blue tracksuit and had a grey towel slung around the back of his stooped neck. He let himself into the bathroom without a word.

Jenny's mood stayed low all through the morning. I escaped the worst of it by shutting myself in the box-room and working on a new study pack that had been waiting for me when I'd checked the post downstairs in the morning. Every so often Jenny put her head around the door and offered to make more coffee, but I was jumpy enough without it.

At twelve she interrupted again to find out if I was ready for lunch. I told her I was and finished the paragraph I was reading while she lingered in the doorway, watching. Do you think she'll be back for lunch? she asked.

She might eat out. She didn't say she'd be back.

It's just I don't know whether to make enough for two or three.

Well, just make enough for three and we can eat a little

extra if she doesn't come.

I know. I know it's not a problem. I was just wondering if she'd be back for it, that's all.

She's just gone for a walk. That's not a problem either, is it?

No. It's not. I don't know. I just feel bad. I don't want to feel hurt. Or angry with her. I don't want to spoil things, or I know I might never see her again.

You won't spoil things. She's not a child.

Jenny frowned. No, I know, she said. I don't know why I feel like this. But I do. So that's that.

Well, Christ, Jen. It's nothing.

She nodded absently, yawning, suddenly seeming far away and not bothered at all. Maybe I'm just tired. These last two weeks... I'm not sleeping well. She rubbed her face with both hands.

Well, if you're not sleeping you must be tired.

Maybe I'm just hungry. Maybe that's it. Anyway, are you ok?

Yes, I said, trying to sound surprised that she should ask. I'm fine. I fixed my eyes on the page in front of me. There was a fingerprint where I'd been touching the paper and I realised my hands were sweating right to the fingertips.

Come through then, she said.

We ate lunch without saying much. Michael was sleeping soundly in his cot for once and Jenny seemed content to enjoy the peace and quiet. Now that I could see her in the full daylight from the window I realised she looked not tired but exhausted. Her face was puffy as if it hadn't woken up yet; her eyelids hooded down low each time she looked up from her soup dish and swallowed.

At around one there were footsteps on the stairs and along our corridor and Jenny twisted round in her chair to face the door. But it must have been either Alex home on his lunch break or the new tenant I'd passed earlier because no one knocked or came in and Jenny turned away again, unsettled.

Let's put the news on, she said once we'd finished. I want to see the weather – they said earlier there may be storms blowing in.

I switched on the set and turned the volume low enough not to carry through to Michael. Jenny watched it but her eyes kept drifting from the TV to some other place: the magnets on the door of the mini-fridge, or one of Michael's toys left lying on the floor.

Are you still upset? I asked, immediately regretting it because I couldn't keep an irritable edge out of my voice.

She drooped her head and sighed. Just ignore me. I don't know what's wrong with me. I just need to pull myself together. Christine can't help being odd, can she? She just didn't have a normal childhood or adolescence or anything. God knows what damage that man did to her. All those years under his influence. All those lies. I'm just lucky I got away. Oh God, she said. It's not too late, is it Luke?

I didn't know what to say, so said nothing.

She straightened her neck, then let her head tilt back and closed her eyes. I could see the forked vein at the side of her neck ticking under the taut skin.

I turned away. I'll wash up, I said. Tell me what the weather report says, if I miss it.

I will, she said, and brought her head swinging forward. I'm watching properly now.

The sink in the kitchen was loaded with debris. Someone had cooked porridge, burned it stuck onto a big steel pan and left it to soak in cold water. Then they'd dumped what seemed like a week's load of crusted up plates and cutlery on top of it. Tucked down the side was an ancient baking tray with a burned pie base soldered to it. Where the pastry hadn't burned black it was swollen and ready to break up in the water. It looked like dead flesh and when I delved into the bowl a smell like cat food rose up from the meat left clinging to it. Alex, I thought, though of course it might have been anyone on the upper floors. I remembered Christine's drunken, knowing scorn in the bar. I hauled enough of the crockery out to give me room to rinse the soup plates and spoons under the hot tap. I swilled them through quickly, dried them and stowed them away.

When I got back to Jenny I thought she was sleeping, but she opened her eyes when I got close. The TV was still on but the news and weather had finished and Neighbours was playing, the volume so low I could hardly hear a word.

Storms on the weekend, Jenny said, then yawned. What time do you have to go?

About half two.

She looked at her watch but didn't comment.

Why don't you sleep for a while?

She shook her head. I don't like to sleep in the day. You know I never can, anyway. It makes me depressed.

You could lie on the sofa and just rest. You don't have to sleep.

She yawned again. Maybe, she said. Will you lie down with me? Just for a while?

Ok, I said.

Do you mind?

No, no. I've finished reading.

She rose stiffly out of the chair and moved to the sofa where she arranged a couple of cushions as pillows. Then she half sat, half lay and swung her legs up to settle full length on her side.

I went to switch the TV off but she called me back. Don't, she said. Leave it on low. I like the voices in the background.

I left it and stretched out alongside her, facing her, my chin resting against her forehead. I laid one arm over her body and tucked the other between our chests. I could feel her heart tapping at the back of my hand.

Are you comfortable like that? she asked. Your arm's not trapped?

I told her it was fine, and gradually she seemed to relax. Don't let me sleep, she mumbled, and soon she was gone, breathing small unconscious breaths into the hollow of my neck.

For a while I listened to the television running behind my back, then felt my own eyelids getting heavy and knew I should wake Jenny and sit up in case I slept past two. Part of me wanted to give in, though – the thought of meeting Christine was like a stone inside and the easiest way was to let it pin me there on the sofa, like some blind, deaf creature on the seabed, until the time to make decisions was over.

Lying still and letting my thoughts drift to anything except Christine, a memory came into my head from a bible reading I'd heard at a cousin's funeral when I was sixteen or so – just after I'd started my apprenticeship at the pit. He'd died in a hit-and-run, walking home drunk in the middle of the road between Pontypridd and Glyncoch. It was from the Old Testament somewhere, about some prophet who raised a boy from the dead. The prophet laid himself full-length on top of the corpse – mouth to mouth, toe to toe – and the boy revived. I hadn't known my cousin very well at all, and grew bored and uncomfortable on the hard chapel pew as the minister spun out the story, but it came back to me with a sudden, weird clarity as I lay there on the sofa with Jenny, feeling her weight on my arm and her breath on my bare throat.

I think that maybe I would have lain there long past two, or even three, or four, letting memories and half-dreams wash over me, and everything then would have been different – all the years between then and now – but suddenly, maybe at some small movement I made, or some change in my breathing, Jenny was awake and stretching her straight, warm body. She turned her open face up to mine, and I knew then I'd have to go.

My head didn't clear much until I opened the front door onto the prom and a slap of cold air hit me fresh off the sea. I breathed deep and took the steps two at a time. Suddenly all my anxiety and confusion seemed to be working inside me like a fuel – as I walked I could feel the soles of my trainers pushing strong and supple against the pavement as if their rubber was muscle, and part of me. My stomach still felt loaded with a sense of premonition, but now instead of pinning me the weight of it was bowling me forward.

Anzani was serving behind the counter when I got to the shop. He was attending to an old man who seemed to be quizzing him about something. When he saw me waiting he called over to a girl labelling tins on the shelves and said, this gentleman wants to know about our pies. Show him what we have, okay? Excuse me, he said to the old guy.

The girl started pointing out the pies and describing each filling. She spoke to the pensioner in a slow, sing-song voice which he seemed to like. He grinned toothily at her.

Hey Luke, come out the back, eh? He led me through the shop and out into a damp concrete yard. The van was parked in front of a row of steel refuse bins. Anzani opened the van door, made way for me to climb in, and pointed out the indicator and switches. She's all loaded up, he said. The delivery list is on the dashboard there, ok?

I nodded and took the keys off him.

Ok, he said. First place is the Maltsters Arms. You know it, eh?

Opposite the station?

Good. Ok. Then a few places out of town. Nothing too far away though. He seemed a bit nervous now, regretting letting me loose in his van, maybe. And when you finish, leave it at the warehouse and keep the keys for tomorrow. He took one last look inside the cab. Ok, he said again. He slammed the door and watched me draw the seat belt across my chest and buckle it before unbolting and swinging open the whitewashed wooden gates.

I started the engine and eased out past Anzani, conscious of him studying me through the cab window. The yard gave onto a narrow back street I didn't recognise. It was empty so I turned right and started figuring out the best way to get around the one-way system to the library.

Christine was waiting on the steps. She smiled thinly

and didn't say anything other than a quick hello as she clambered up into the passenger seat and heaved the door shut behind her.

Sorry – I'm a bit late, I said, wanting to start some kind of conversation.

Don't worry. I didn't notice.

I turned the van, with some difficulty, holding up a line of waiting drivers, and headed back towards the town centre. Are you sure you want to do this? I asked. I haven't driven for years. I can hardly remember where the clutch is.

Of course I want to. It's fine. I feel safe with you.

I looked at her, surprised, almost trundling through a junction. I kicked down at the brake and we both pitched forward. Sorry. Put your belt on, I said.

So. Where are we going? She looked straight ahead as she spoke. It made me even more nervous than I already was. I could feel my palms slipping on the smooth plastic of the wheel.

A pub near the station.

Where then?

Don't know. Have a look for me. I reached for the clipboard holding the delivery list and handed it to her, hoping she wouldn't notice the rash of sweat my hand had left on the wheel.

Ok, she said, and took it from me, brushing her fingers briefly against mine. I've bought a map, she added, and she was looking at me at last now and smiling.

A map?

Of the whole area. In case we go out of town to somewhere you don't know the way to. She studied the schedule. We've only got four places after this, she said, disappointed.

Where are they?

Three more in town, I think, then one in some place I can't make out. She stared closer at the clipboard. His handwriting's awful, she said. Anyway, it's a Welsh name starting with a 'P' or a 'D'. I can't tell.

I'll check when we get to the pub.

Then I'll look it up on my new map.

I wasn't sure if she meant it to sound comical. I couldn't decide if this new, child-like mood was a real attempt at intimacy or just some extended sardonic joke. When I glanced across to check her expression she kept her head bowed, eyes fixed on the clipboard, her fingers toying with the cheap yellow biro someone had attached to it with Sellotape and string.

The deliveries around town were straightforward enough – boxes of snacks, crates of bottled beers and a few trays of shrink-wrapped pies. The out of town address turned out to be in a village called Penderyn, though, which was ten miles inland and on a route I'd never taken before. Christine seemed genuinely pleased to have to use her map and she read out each direction in a precise, military kind of way hundreds of yards before I actually reached any of the junctions.

The village was small – just a single terraced street with bigger, manse-like houses separated off – and the hotel we needed was impossible to miss. I pulled up at the kerb outside the main door, which was shut. There was a bell in the shallow porch, but ringing it didn't do any good. After a couple of minutes I looked back at Christine and shrugged.

Tap the windows, she called.

The glass was frosted except where the lettering for the hotel's name, The Red Dragon, had been stencilled and left clear. I looked through the lettering but it was gloomy inside and the glass was dirty. I tapped a few times anyway but wasn't surprised when nobody came. The day had been overcast, but now a late afternoon burst of sun was warming the back of my neck. I looked up and down the street but apart from a young mother hauling two kids towards me there was nothing stirring. I'll go round the back, I told Christine, and she nodded, one hand raised up now to shield her eyes from the new glare.

There was an alleyway running along the side of the hotel and off it a wider lane with back entrances to all the buildings on the main street. The wooden door to the hotel's back yard was ajar so I pushed it and walked in. The few wooden tables and a set of children's swings were completely deserted. A muddy Land Rover occupied one of the spaces in the car park and a rusty bicycle stood propped against one of the posts holding up an empty washing line. Nothing stirred and I was considering giving up and leaving the delivery piled high on the pavement when a fire escape door clattered and scraped open on the first floor. A short fat woman in a white apron appeared on the metal balcony. Yes? she snapped.

I've got a delivery round the front, I called up.

Yes – deliveries round the front!

I shrugged up at her. I knocked, I said, but I couldn't get an answer.

Well. You will now. She waved me back out of the yard, disappeared inside and dragged the fire door shut behind her. The sound of its steel bar locking into place cracked like a gunshot and somewhere along the lane a dog started to bark.

By the time I got back round to the front door it was open, though there was still no one around. I shifted the boxes and crates inside, stacking them on the balding hall carpet. Hello! That's the delivery in! I called when I'd finished, but got no answer. I waited a few seconds, then wandered back outside and opened the van door. Did you see where she went? I asked Christine. I need her to sign for it.

She shook her head, unclipped her seat belt and got out of the cab to join me on the pavement. She hooked her thumbs into the back pockets of her jeans and flexed her upper body, arching back from the waist.

We can't go until someone signs the bloody invoice, I said.

She tilted her head, amused, and squinted at me. Let's go inside.

There was a broad staircase just a little way along the hall. Christine sauntered halfway up its stairs, then turned and grinned at me. She carried on out of sight, turning onto a landing running over my head. Within a few moments a door opened and closed somewhere on the floor she was on, but not in the direction she'd gone. Christine, I called as low as I could, and started after her up the stairs.

There was a flurry of light footsteps and suddenly Christine was back on the stairs and skipping past me back to the van. The fat woman arrived on the landing in time to see the back of Christine's head, maybe, but nothing else. You only need to ring the bell, she scolded. That's all you need to do, you know. I've got a thousand and one things to see to. I can't be everywhere. A man's voice – low and bad-tempered – rolled along the upstairs corridor from somewhere behind her. She stumped down the stairs, snatched the clipboard off me and signed without even glancing at the delivery. There, she said. Now off these stairs.

Sorry, I said, and retreated to the door.

There, she said again. The bell, there. See?

Look, said Christine, when I got back into the cab and started the engine. She drew a big glass ashtray out from under her jacket. It had the sign of the hotel etched in red on its base.

Where the hell did you get that?

One of the bedrooms. The door was open.

Jesus, I said. Why?

She shrugged. It must have been a nice place once, if they had their own ashtrays. Don't you think?

I don't believe it, I said. What the hell were you thinking?

It's just an ashtray, she said, and studied it more carefully. I'm sure they had lots of them. It's clean, she added, as if that was what might be bothering me.

All the way back to town Christine hummed quietly to herself; scraps of classical music, then what sounded like hymns and choruses. The sun stayed bright and by the time we hit the rush-hour traffic my forehead was throbbing.

Where are we going? she asked when I turned off from the main route into the centre.

They were the first words she'd spoken to me since showing me the ashtray and I could feel my blood swarming up. I took a deep breath to control my voice. Anzani wanted the van left at the warehouse.

It'll be nice to see where you work, she said, as casually as if we'd been chatting happily for miles. She was looking away again, humming another hymn. It sounded familiar though I couldn't place it and thought it might be a Christmas carol, or something I used to hear in Sunday School when I was a kid. I turned back to the road and soon was easing the van into the sharp corner at the bottom of the warehouse hill. It's up this road, I told her, just for something to say.

She broke off her tune. I've walked this way, she said. I remember how steep this hill was, and going down the other side to the castle and the seafront. She turned to face me. Maybe you were in the warehouse when I walked past.

I nodded, the hairs on the back of my neck bristling like pins. Here we are, I said, pulling the van over onto the concrete apron fronting the warehouse doors. An awkward silence fell over us once I'd killed the engine. For a while we both just sat still, waiting, though for what I didn't know.

Take me inside the warehouse, she said at last, and those must have been the words I was waiting for somewhere in my mind because I wasn't surprised and the answer came straight to my lips.

I can't, I lied. I've only got the keys for the van, not the door. Sorry. I unclipped my seat belt, suddenly embarrassed at having apologised.

It doesn't matter, she said.

While I locked the van, Christine wandered up to the side door of the warehouse. She squatted and lifted the letterbox to peer through.

There's nothing to see, I told her.

She straightened up and shrugged. Too dark to tell, anyway.

I looked up and down the road. Which way do you want to walk home?

Up the hill.

The sun was weaker now and a cool, marine atmosphere had begun to settle in the early evening shadows. A strip of bright sunshine still lit the opposite side of the road but Christine seemed content to stay in the shade. She set off quickly and in a few minutes we were clear of the buildings and amongst steep slopes of broom and gorse. What's up there? she asked, pausing for breath.

The golf course.

Do you get a good view up on top? She swept her hair back. Do you get a view of the castle and the sea? Her face was starting to pink with warmth.

I told her yes, but didn't start climbing again. I looked up at the gorse bushes and the faint, sandy ways between them and waited again like I'd waited in the van.

Let's climb up – I'd like to see. She was already walking so I followed her, watching her haunches work under the denim.

About halfway up the hill she took one of the side-trails, easing through overhanging gorse and broom, and as if by instinct brought us to the patch of open grass where I'd often sat to be alone and eat olives and drink a beer between the end of a shift and the slow walk home. I noticed an empty olive jar, almost hidden in the tangle of gorse roots where I'd left it months before.

What's that? Christine said. She'd stopped and was waiting for me.

Nothing, I said. I used to come up here for a break

sometimes, that's all. I must have left an empty jar behind one day. I pointed it out with the toe of my shoe.

She stooped down to see. There's a beer bottle, too, she said to me over her shoulder. She sounded pleased, and bent to pick it up. There's a dead slug in it, she reported.

They like beer.

It's just a little one. She flipped the bottle and its passenger deeper into the gorse bush.

I looked back down over the tops of the bushes, towards the warehouse. The zinc roof and the flat top of the tyre-fitters were shining like brass in the reddish, angled light.

It's peaceful here.

I turned and saw she'd sat down now, knees drawn up to her chest. I thought about the last time I'd wandered up this way, watching black, long-legged flies reeling from blossom to blossom. There were no flies now, just a heavy-looking bee drowsing into the sharp heart of the bushes. The memory seemed strange – vivid but remote – like something I'd dreamed I'd once done. I sat down next to her, and I didn't know if what I felt was a kind of excitement or despair. My arms felt numb and useless, trembling, too heavy to support, and I folded them over my raised knees.

I had to go to counselling, you know, she said. I was in a bad way after the funeral, and things happened, and the doctors at the hospital made me speak to people. Shrinks, you know?

What kinds of things?

She shook her head. They were all so stupid. It was like living with my mother and Jenny again. They couldn't tell me why I should feel one thing for somebody and not another thing. You can only be one thing to somebody you love, they said, but they couldn't tell me why I couldn't be more than one thing, if I wanted to be. If it was my choice. It was too late by then, but they still couldn't tell me. Just legal things, and second hand psychology. Babble babble babble. They were like the kids I teach: full of silly rules they don't even understand. So I just told them what they wanted to hear, and they said I was getting better. I don't have to talk to them anymore.

Your father? I said.

You don't know what it's like to be told that you can't possibly love the person you love most in the world, and that the love you feel for them is part of being damaged, and wrong. You have no idea.

No, I said. I don't.

She was silent for a while. The Bible says, Know ye not that we shall judge angels? He liked that. I think it was his favourite verse. It was in the letter he left me, too. I never showed the letter to anyone.

You seem to know what you think, I said. And what you feel. That's something.

She nodded, absently. The last time you were in this place, you didn't even know what I looked like, she said, and her voice was low and drowsy. Everything else was the same, but you didn't know who I was. You'd only just found out I existed. That's right, isn't it?

Yes, I said. I could barely speak.

How can such a simple truth change everything? But change is always simple. I sometimes think now that if I'd been walking the fields on Pugh's farm, or passing by the whins above the warehouse, and God's still, small voice had come from a burning bush the way it came to Moses, the way Christine's came to me that day, I would have obeyed without doubting it, and without surprise. And why not? I ask myself now, after half a lifetime spent wondering. We're all believers for as long as we sleep, and nothing we dream is strange until we wake. And maybe that's just how they happen, the big, irrevocable changes in our lives, underneath their dull material facts. We go through the looking glass, we wrestle the angel, we stumble on the goddess bathing naked. We hear the voice that tells us to sacrifice our son, and we pretend we have all kinds of answers to it, reasonable and human, but maybe all we have is Abraham's weary Here I am.

It's like I'd just been born, in your mind, she said. She moved her face to mine and before I had time to even register what was happening we were kissing, hard and clumsy. I pulled her on top of me, felt her grind herself against my thigh and raised it, forcing her legs wider. Straining, I worked an arm between us and found the button of her jeans, opened it and tugged at the zip. She gasped as I drove my fingers lower, jamming them between denim and skin, finding the thin cotton underneath. I heard myself moaning at the back of my throat but kept my mouth clamped to hers. Raising my thigh again I lifted her closer so that her whole weight was bearing down on me. I thrust up and suddenly her mouth left mine to fasten at my neck.

No! I said, in a voice that didn't seem to belong to me. Don't mark me.

She rolled away as if she'd been kicked. She was breathing quick and shallow but not with passion. Something else.

I stared at her, touching my throat, not knowing what to say.

Someone's coming, she said simply, and buttoned and zipped her jeans before jumping to her feet.

I hadn't heard a thing but she was right – two young boys puffed by on the far side of the bushes, loaded golf bags slung over their backs. They glanced at us through a break in the gorse, then gave each other a look.

We should get back, Christine said matter-of-factly once they'd passed. She bent to kiss me lightly on the cheek then started back ahead of me down the slope.

The rest of the walk home passed in a blur. If we spoke at all, I can't remember anything of it. When we reached Bethesda she said she wanted to see the basement kitchen. You said you'd show me, she said. The day I arrived.

I know, I said, remembering.

I led her past the Clements' flat. The mumble of a TV show and the chinking of cutlery came from behind the closed door and just for a moment filled me with a kind of loneliness. I had the feeling that some kind of rescue was waiting, there in their stuffy living room of television shows, small talk, knitting, and dinners on trays, but we were already past the door and heading down the basement stairs.

The enormous kitchen was empty. Christine surveyed it for a few seconds, then wandered up along the side of the long bench table, staring at the iron hobs ranged along the walls. When she came back to me she ran her open hand up my forearm, stroking it without closing her fingers. I almost reached for her, but held myself back.

What's in there? she said softly, looking past me, back through the kitchen doorway.

A dining room. I turned to face it.

She left my side and walked to its glass-panelled door. She peered in. Everything's covered with cloths, she said. All the tables. You can see the shapes of glasses and dishes under them. It's horrible.

I moved behind her and put my hands around her waist. She didn't move them.

It's like in old films where rooms have been left because someone's died in them, she went on. She pressed her forehead to the glass, staring deeper into the unlit room.

I got myself locked in there once, I said.

She stayed turned to the glass. How?

There'd been storms and high tides and they'd had to take the floor up in the far corner. I wandered in to look around because I'd never seen the door open before. Anyway, the next thing I knew the key was turning in the lock.

Why didn't you shout?

Too embarrassed. We hadn't long moved in and I didn't want Clement thinking I'd been snooping, or trying to thieve something. In the end I climbed through one of those little half windows into the yard. I pointed to the windows through the glass. They didn't look much bigger than cat-flaps from where we were standing now and it was strange to think of hauling myself through one of them.

You fitted through one of those?

I laughed and nodded. Despite what had happened, and was happening between us, I was enjoying telling her the story. Then, I said, I had to get past Clement's old Alsatian in the yard. He actually bit me on the arse as I climbed the wall.

Christine half turned her head against my chest. Did

they ever find out?

No, I don't think so. They never said anything, anyway.

She leaned back a little more strongly against me, but now I'd spoken about it I found my mind drifting back to what I'd seen in the room after the storms. Where the floorboards had been pulled away there was a space around a foot deep, then sand and shingle. In the bad light it seemed colourless – a kind of ghost beach. I was startled to see it there, stretching off into the shadows. It struck me that it must all have been lying there, sand and pebbles and bleached shells, since the buildings went up more than a century before – a buried, silent night-beach running under half the town. I remember dreaming about it not long afterwards and waking up convinced that my father, wherever he was now, had died in the night while I slept.

Christine levered the cheap gilt door handle and pushed, but it was locked as usual and didn't budge. Why are you living here? she asked.

I almost laughed. It's not so bad, is it?

She shrugged and let go of the handle. Her free hand drifted back to the side of my thigh, stroking it gently.

My chest felt too tight with her weight against it, and I wanted to breathe deep to take the pressure off, but didn't want her to think it was a sigh. Instead I slipped the tips of my fingers under the tight waistband of her jeans and she drew her stomach in, making space. I slid both hands deeper, till my knuckles caught, and she breathed out to trap them there.

Footsteps tramped on the staircase over our heads. Students, I said, and let her go.

She rearranged her shirt, tucking it back neatly into her

jeans. Without speaking we made our way past the two girls on the stairs and up to the flat.

Jenny went out of her way all through that evening to be cheerful and to make up with Christine. She'd made a big pasta bake for when we got in and announced it as soon as we came through the door. I remembered you saying you liked Italian food, she told her sister.

Christine seemed calm and quietly cheerful and that helped me keep my own mood up, though whenever they were out of my sight together my stomach went into a guilty, fearful cramp.

At the table Christine chatted brightly about the hotel we couldn't get into and the fat, fierce woman there. Afterwards she helped with Michael and then with the dishes after Jenny suggested they left him with me while they saw to the kitchen.

For the endless minutes they were gone I paced the flat's two rooms with Michael lodged like a deadweight in my arms. I dreaded Jenny's return, imagining her broken by some tearful confession, but at the same time craved Christine's presence whatever the circumstance.

But there was no confession, and once they were back the time passed quickly – they laughed together over simple things and drank more of the wine I fetched from the basement.

Later still, in bed at night, I lay restless and hard – *Go and see,* she'd said, that day on the beach; *go and see* – until Jenny, sensing something, turned to me and ran her small hands over my body, bit my face and neck, chest and sides, nipping and breathing onto the pinked flesh. She can sense the new life in me, I remember thinking with a kind of horror, even as I rolled towards her and lifted myself, then drew her to her knees; she can sense the new life and she thinks it's for her.

Nine

It wasn't until mid-morning of the next day that Christine mentioned Bill Kerrigan's party. She'd swum for longer that day, and Jenny had begun to get nervous, waking me and insisting I get dressed in case of some emergency. The wind had picked up earlier than usual and every few minutes she'd drifted to the window to check on the choppiness of the sea.

When Christine did return her mood had changed from the evening before. She wasn't high now, though an air of contentment, maybe a kind of triumph, still surrounded her when she smiled or spoke. It unnerved me, and maybe at some deep level it unsettled Jenny, too, though she couldn't have known why.

I didn't know if you'd still want to go, Jenny said to neither of us in particular, and it fell between us awkwardly. We had a nice time last night just the three of us, didn't we?

I'd like to, Christine said at last. I've been looking forward to it.

Jenny shrugged and sucked at a nail she'd been biting.

Do you still want to go, Luke? Christine fixed me with a wide open, innocent look.

I don't mind. I'm happy to go if you want to.

There was silence for a while. That's fine, then, Jenny said at last, and clamped her fingers between her thighs like that was the only way she could keep from tearing them to the bone.

Christine unwound herself out of her chair and padded through to Michael's cot. She'd come down from her shower barefoot, wearing just a faded cotton shift that seemed in some simple, unabashed way to make her body seem more naked than if it were bare. He was banging a toy at the bars and I heard her baby-talk to him, then lift him out. I glanced at Jenny but she resisted calling her sister through or turning to watch her. She closed her eyes and cocked her head instinctively, listening like a wild animal or bird.

In the afternoon I had a three-hour warehouse shift and it kept me mindlessly busy – there were four deliveries to wait on and though none of the stock was too heavy it was hard, repetitive work shuttling between the lorries and the warehouse stacks.

On the way home I had nothing to keep my mind off the fact that Jenny and Christine had spent hours together, talking, and so I felt no surprise, just a kind of sickened resignation, when I heard the muffled sounds of a quarrel from behind the flat door. It wasn't that I imagined Christine feeling remorse for what we'd done, and for what seemed to be happening between us, but that some kind of crisis, some kind of release was simply the next unavoidable stage on the path I was suddenly and haplessly stumbling along, like a sleepwalker following a voice in a dream, and nearing the top of the stairs.

I waited in the corridor for a few minutes, but couldn't make out any words. Finally I put my key to the lock, turned it and walked in.

Just don't then! That's all! Just don't! I heard Jenny yell. Then: Luke, she said, catching sight of me stood in the doorway. Her voice fell quiet, like a switch had been flicked inside her. She was holding Michael tight to her chest, and in an instant I knew the quarrel was over him and nothing to do with me at all.

Christine didn't turn to acknowledge me. She was sat rigid on the edge of the sofa, her back straight but shoulders narrowed up like she was flinching from a blow.

What's going on? I said, hearing my voice like a stranger's.

Jenny shook her head without answering. She lowered Michael a few inches and pressed her lips against the crown of his head. Nothing, she said at last, raising her lips from his hair, but keeping her face bowed. It wasn't anything, was it, Chris?

Christine shrugged stiffly.

Well, I said awkwardly, I'll make coffee. Who wants one?

Jenny shook her head again and Christine simply ignored me.

Despite the tension, as I turned to go my whole body felt flooded with relief, as if a blood transfusion had drained me in seconds and now was pumping me full again. The problem with Michael, whatever it was, just felt like one of the poisons about to be irrigated out. I took the stairs to the kitchen in bounds and drank my coffee there, my whole body quivering. I gave Jenny and Christine twenty minutes, then went back down to them.

We spent the early evening staring at the TV. Michael, maybe anxious at the tension in the air, cried miserably for hours in Jenny's arms until the effort sent him into a restless sleep.

At nine, Christine got up and took hold of a cotton

dress she'd left hanging behind the door. I'll get changed in the bedroom, she said to no one in particular, then went through and closed the door behind her.

Jenny looked at me and opened her mouth, but after a pause let it close again without saying a word.

I won't go if you don't want me to, I said. I'm not bothered.

Go, she said. It doesn't matter. We can't spend much longer sitting like this.

What happened earlier? I murmured, listening for the bedroom door. What's going on?

Nothing.

It didn't sound like nothing.

She looked over at the bedroom door, as if Christine might suddenly fling it open and confront her. We spoke about things, she said in a quiet monotone. She's more disturbed than I thought. She's in trouble, Luke. In her mind, I mean. She's so angry. I don't want her near Michael.

I stared at her and she turned away, and I knew she was ashamed. What are you talking about? What's it got to do with Michael?

I don't want her near any of us. Not until she's better. She's ill, Luke. She needs to get better. I can't help her. I thought I could help her because I'm her sister, but I can't. She doesn't want me and she doesn't want help. She wants... I don't know what she wants. I could feel it, she said, close to tears suddenly. I could feel it, and now I know.

What are you talking about? I said. What could you feel?

She shook her head. It doesn't matter. She has to leave

tomorrow. I've told her. That's that.

Christ, I said.

She closed her eyes, lifted a hand and pinched the bridge of her nose like she was stopping a bleed. We talked about it while you were upstairs.

I sank back into the sofa, not wanting Jenny to see my face. I dragged a lungful of air down, silently. Michael squirmed awake and that gave me time to think of some kind of response while she calmed him.

Jenny, just tell me what's going on.

Don't –

The door opened and Christine stepped through. Her eyes were red and puffy from crying. Bedroom's free, she said. I'll go up to the bathroom to finish my make-up.

I gave Jenny a last look, which she didn't meet, then nodded to Christine and went through to get changed.

On the walk to Kerrigan's house, as we made our way up behind Bethesda into narrow Victorian terraces and then up again to the broader, leafier streets in the northeast side of town, I asked Christine what had gone on that afternoon. For a while I thought she wouldn't answer, but when she did her voice was bright and confident, though there was a brittleness too which she couldn't quite cover.

I don't want to talk about it now. I want to enjoy the party. I just made Michael a bit frightened – it was an accident. Jennifer overreacted. That's what she always did. She flashed me a grim little smile.

How did you frighten him? I remembered the small stones again, lying there under his face in his sling, but couldn't begin to find the words to ask her about them. It was too late, I realised. It had been too late the moment I found them.

I don't know. I moved too quickly, maybe, she said vaguely. I don't want to talk about it. Can I come with you in the van tomorrow?

Jenny said you're leaving.

I'm your guest now, remember, she said, and a familiar wave of despair came over me, making me pause for breath though the walking was easy. She waited for me to move again, studying my face. I've been thinking about what happened yesterday, she said.

What have you thought? My legs felt heavy as logs but I forced them to move forward again anyway. I reached out and took her hand but she just squeezed the fingers and let it go.

I like babies, she said, changing the subject. Jennifer wasn't fair.

She's just protective. Michael's her first child. She's bound to be nervous with him.

She wasn't fair. But it doesn't matter – she never was. I've been remembering that. I've been doing a lot of remembering. She looked around her like she wanted to get her bearings. Are we nearly there yet?

Just up this hill. I glanced sideways at her. She was stepping quick and smooth, back straight like it had been on the sofa earlier, eyes fixed dead ahead now.

Chris, why did you and Jenny quarrel? I said, and stopped, but she walked on, only slowing and turning back to check on me halfway along the row of big, detached houses.

Which number? she called.

I caught up with her and led the way through Kerrigan's gate and along his gravelled front path.

It's a lovely house, she said when we got to the porch.

It's all split into student flats. All the houses round here are.

The big front door was off the latch. Music was thumping from somewhere inside. I swung the door open and she stepped past me into the hall.

We followed the music to Kerrigan's sitting room. It was dimly lit and the air was loaded with smoke. About a dozen figures were sprawled around the floor – mainly students but a few older guests too. One of them, a lean, toothy, crop-headed man who I recognised as one of Jenny's old tutors, lifted a can of lager to acknowledge me. I'd spoken to him once or twice at parties like this, in the months after Jenny's graduation. I picked my way over to him and Christine followed behind. He was sat in front of one of the tall speakers and as I took a place next to him I could feel the bass vibrating at the back of my head. It was impossible to speak, which suited me. He reached behind him for two cans and offered them to us. I took one but Christine shook her head and sat staring at the bodies scattered around her.

Kerrigan was nowhere to be seen, but after a few minutes I looked up to see him coming through the door with a couple of bottles of wine. For a few moments he stood surveying the scene, grinning into the warm fog, his eyes passing over me blank as washers. A girl said something to him as she passed by, leaving the room, and he nodded, put the bottles on the floor and came straight towards us. I lifted a hand to greet him, but all he wanted to do was turn the music a little lower and when he did catch my eye he looked surprised to see me, but nodded and smiled. Luke, he barked above the music, you know

Graham? He gestured to the man beside me and I nodded. Good, he said. He glanced at Christine, then swayed off toward a cluster of students in the far corner.

Now that I'd been reminded of his name I turned to Graham. How are things? I shouted.

He turned the music lower still. Sorry, he said. I recognise the face, but...

Luke, I said. I met you a couple of times with Jenny. She was in a few of your classes. A couple of years back.

He nodded. That's right. Sorry. I think I've seen you round the library, too?

Probably, I said. I use it now and again. I'm doing some courses with the OU.

Ah, he said. He took a nip from a skinny rollup he'd been cradling between his bony knees. So how's Jenny getting on? She's got a baby now, I heard.

Yes. They're both doing fine.

Do you see her often?

I laughed. We're married, I said, raising my voice to carry over the crashing opening riff to a new song.

Christ! he said. Sorry! He peered at me more closely and took another drag. You don't look old enough, he laughed.

I turned to Christine but she was gone and when I scanned the room for her I could only make out the same knots of people that had been there when we came in. I drained my can, got up and signalled to Graham that I was off to get more beer. He gave me a thumbs up, looking bored now and ready to drink all he could get his hands on.

She was in the kitchen – a huge cold room at the back of the flat – sitting at Kerrigan's farmhouse table with Kerrigan himself. Behind them a few students were perched on stools around the tall fridge, passing a couple of wine boxes from knee to knee, plastic cup to plastic cup. I helped myself to a brace of four-packs from the fridge, then stood beside her at the table. She looked up at me, stony-faced, as if I were a stranger. I could sense Kerrigan's eyes on me, and his mild irritation, and despite the coolness of the kitchen my scalp started to prick with sweat.

What? she said.

I fixed my eyes on Kerrigan, trying to block her from my mind so I could maybe salvage the situation. Sorry to butt in. Jenny said to say hello.

I'm sorry she couldn't come, he said. Would've been good to see her. It's been a while. He looked at the beers in my hand and I was suddenly conscious of not having brought anything.

Well. Catch you later, I said.

Yeah.

I made my way to Graham again and dropped beside him, handing him one of the packs.

Cheers, he said. I found rum, he went on, and showed me a halflitre he'd hidden behind the speaker.

Last time I was here I stole his good whisky, I said.

His body rocked approvingly.

I'm not sure how long I sat there drinking – hours on end, it seemed. Far on in the night I remember another lecturer who Jenny had once introduced me to – a square, tough-faced American woman called Dr Case – stumping over to Graham and complaining about the amount of dope being smoked in the room. She didn't recognise me, so I just sat further back alongside the speaker, closed my eyes and listened to the white noise of the party swilling around me. I was helping Graham with the rum by then and at some point I remember crawling slowly past

Graham's raised knees, pulling myself upright alongside an armchair and falling onto the couple who were locked blind together in it. The next thing I remember is stumbling into an empty bedroom and sitting on a wooden-backed chair in the dark, hoping absurdly that Christine would come and find me there.

Finally, in a daze of resentment and jealousy, I made my way back to the kitchen. The party seemed to have thinned out and there were only two people there now, a young woman and an older man, slumped facing each other across the debris of glasses, empty cans and ashtrays littering the table. They were smoking and talking earnestly in low tones, the man shaking his head slowly and continuously.

Do you know where Bill is? I broke in.

Who? the girl demanded, annoyed at being interrupted.

Bill Kerrigan. You know, the guy whose party it is.

No. I don't know him. Anyway, what fucking party, eh?

He was here in the kitchen but he's gone, the man said, slurring. He went into the garden with some other people. He'll be in with the music and stuff, now, maybe. I don't know.

The garden was empty, but the cold night air cleared my head a little and I stayed outside for a few minutes, breathing it in and looking up at the stars between heavy, dragging clouds. A thin grey cat pressed itself against my shin, startling me. It mewed, staring up at my face, then padded across the big, untidy lawn and disappeared in the shadows.

Back inside I found them in the sitting room, not far from where I'd been slumped against the wall earlier.

They'd stopped talking now and Christine looked tired and distracted. All the anger in me lifted away and it was all I could do to stop myself crossing the room sitting abject at her feet in relief. Instead I edged my way around the wall towards them.

She turned when I tapped her shoulder and gave me a thin smile. Where have you been? I'd like to go soon, she said.

I nodded. There was no music in the room now, just scattered, drunken conversation. The woman who'd spoken to Kerrigan earlier and told him to turn the music down was picking her way over outstretched legs and prone bodies, gathering bottles and crushed cans into a black plastic sack. One of his flatmates, I guessed. Kerrigan watched her, motionless, his dark eyes hooded and solemn-looking.

Where did it come from, the Sea of Light? I heard somebody chant, and turned to see Graham reading to three prone students from a slim book he must have found on one of the shelves. He repeated the line in Welsh, then went on with the rest of the poem, translating in fragments as the mood took him; something about a huntsman in the rushes between two fields, a field of grass and a field of flowers.

Kerrigan got up from the floor and staggered out to the hall. In the quiet I heard the bathroom door close and the lock snap to.

Let's go now, Christine said. Before he comes back.

The rain began almost as soon as we left the house – cold, fat, Atlantic drops. I don't know when Christine arrived at the decision to make for the rocks and the sea instead of Bethesda – maybe there and then as we hunched under the rain, or maybe while she'd sat and watched the night go by in a swirl of strangers and empty talk, or maybe she'd been planning it all along, for days – but at some point I realised she'd quickened her pace and was heading away from the orange lights of the promenade, toward the dark of the headland.

No – the other way, I called. I was still quite drunk, though the walk had begun to sober me, and when she didn't turn I jogged after her numbly, splashing through puddles, hardly feeling the ground under my feet. I was desperate, almost to the point of weeping, to get back to warmth, familiarity, and the blankness of sleep.

She waited until I'd caught up then said simply: Come with me. Will you?

Where are you going?

Just come with me. We won't be long.

I don't know if I should have turned away and let her go. Would she have given up and followed me? I doubt it. Would she have ever come back again? How could I tell? And of course I'll never know, though I've asked myself the question a thousand times since, when I've woken from dreams in the small hours, almost smelling the rain and sea.

I followed her down to the shingle where the tide was sweeping black and slow, drowning the patter of the rain with its drag and hiss. She stooped to peel away her canvas shoes and carried them barefoot, one in each hand, picking her way carefully onto the smooth rocks above the swilling water. I was frightened for her now, and staying with her as much from a dull, protective instinct as from fascination.

Had Jenny shown her the place where we first met? Where she'd climbed up to me and smiled and offered me wine and company? I think so now, though I didn't know then and will never know for sure. And either way, whether by chance or design, she stopped at the same low, flat rock and lifted her soaked dress over her head, unclipped her bra, rolled down her underwear and lowered herself whitely, waist deep, into the moving water.

I watched in a kind of trance. The rain had stopped and the lights of the town were hidden by the headland. A strange, enormous stillness seemed to have settled on the world – the quiet, lapping sea, shifting in its sleep, and the great blanket of clouds above it, already beginning to pale with the first faint glimmer of morning. She waved me toward her and I undressed, shivering, and joined her.

To begin with I swam in her wake, the gripping cold stealing all my thought from me so that I moved in a kind of strenuous dream, mechanical and slow, keeping pace with the sound of her movements breaking the water ahead of me. My eyes burned with the salt and soon I was swimming blind, eyelids tight shut, conscious only of the lift and drop of each lazy swell. When I felt the first deep tug of the current sweeping out from the bay to the open sea I stopped and turned my body in the water, treading on God knows how many fathoms of nothing, facing the shore again. Christine's head, just visible, bobbed darkly like a seal's in the distance. She was making her way toward the headland now and I realised I must have lost her when she changed direction.

When does one life end and another begin? It was then, I think, for me: watching the far away, shadowy cliffs seem to rise and fall with the swell, a deeper black against the dark sky and its pale stars; treading deep water, feeling the dead chill of it in my blood and bones; all that frigid weight of ocean holding me in its grip. I wasn't afraid, though the last of my drunkenness had soaked away and

I understood with complete clarity the danger I was in; instead, what I was most conscious of was the oddly dream-like impossibility of rest – of my feet stirring listlessly like tiny straws, my arms and hands waving like insect wings in slow motion; I was hovering, and had to keep hovering, dizzyingly high up, pinned above a seabed that stretched like an empty desert all the way to America.

I found Christine waiting for me, dressed again, on the steps of Bethesda. By then it was almost dawn and the rain had begun again, washing the salt from our faces and hair. I could see the deep chill in the blue-white skin of her arms and legs.

What kinds of thoughts had passed through my head between losing her in the dark and finding her there, shivering at the door? They're lost to me now, vanished along with the years; maybe they already were, even as we faced each other. Maybe any attempt at making sense is just a kind of forgetting. Maybe only the story happens, not the meaning. The selkie steps out of the waves, and we think we're the tellers – we think it or we'd go mad – but we're the listeners. No, not even that. We're the thing that's told, and nobody – nothing – is listening.

Inside the door we stood near the radiator at the foot of the stairs for a while, letting the water drip from our hair and clothes. It was too early for the Clements to be stirring, but high above us the flush of a lavatory sent the sound of draining water gurgling faintly through the wall. Neither of us spoke and finally she turned her back on me and started climbing the stairs to the flat. And to Jenny, sleeping, or lying wakeful in the dark.

Ten

When I woke late the next morning, Christine was already gone. I knew without needing to leave the bedroom. The door was ajar and I could hear Jenny speaking to Michael. Her voice was freer and softer: some kind of tension had relaxed and slackened in it. I hadn't noticed consciously that it had changed in the first place, but lying there and listening to her talking half to Michael and half to herself, I realised she suddenly sounded familiar again, and I knew what that meant. Eventually she put her head around the door to check on me. You're awake, she said.

What's the time?

About eleven. What time did you come in?

I don't know. Four or five, maybe. You were asleep.

No. I remember you getting undressed. Your jeans were soaked through and you couldn't get them off.

I tried to smile. I don't remember, I lied.

I want to cook a meal this evening, she announced suddenly. Just for us. To get back to being just us, and everything normal again. She joined me on the bed and lay flat on her back on top of the sheets, staring at the ceiling. There was a calm finality in the way she spoke.

Fine, I said, and kept my eyes fixed on the profile of her face. Her jaw was clenching and unclenching, shifting all the time.

You're going out in the van again today?

God. That's right. I'll need to shift this headache. I

stayed quiet then. I knew better than to mention Christine, though of course she was all I was thinking about. There would be no mention of Christine now, or of her going, at least not this morning, I understood. How far away was she now? Was she already waiting between trains somewhere, staring into a coffee, or watching the land go by through a thick window, angry with me maybe – yes, she'd be angry, it was anger all along – like she'd always been with Jenny. Angry forever. *We won't be long*, she'd said. And then she was naked, white and slim and shivering, stepping into the sea.

I know what happened, Jenny said.

I felt my heart and breathing stop, as if a hand had covered my face, smothering my nose and mouth. Nothing happened, I managed to say.

Don't, she said. I know what happened. You could have died. You could easily have fucking died. You don't even swim very well. She could have killed you. Her voice was cracking now. I thought she might turn and hit out at me, furious, but she caught her breath and steadied her tone. You didn't think about me, or Michael. You didn't think about us. You didn't think how that would have been.

I shook my head. I meant nothing happened between us.

She stared at me then, so long and steadily I had to turn my head at last and look away. That, she said. That never even occurred to me. I don't even know what to say to that. Christ's sake, Luke, she said. She rolled away from me and climbed off the bed.

I didn't know what you were thinking, I said. I closed my eyes.

The phone on the landing started ringing but we both ignored it, waiting for it to be answered or to stop. Nobody went to it, and in the end, mid-trill, it cut off. Through in the living room Michael began to grizzle.

What goes on in your head? Jenny asked as she went through to him, talking to any one of us, maybe – Michael, me or herself.

I collected the van in an exhausted daze, hardly responding when Anzani handed over the delivery list and explained the route. I was going further afield that day: out along the Rheidol Valley in fact, near Pugh's farm, to some of the small tourist shops, pubs and cafes around Devil's Bridge. The weather had worsened by the time I walked the mile or so around the bay to the shop, as if the equinox had shifted and brought its big, planetary storms ahead of time, and now we stood hunched over a map together, in the narrow shelter of the back porch, the rain jumping up from the concrete. He circled each stop with a biro, the hiss of the rain almost drowning out his words even if I'd been listening to them. The yard stank and in the nearest corner a pile of sodden debris had been raked together and heaped up – last year's black leaves belched up by the drains, silt, scraps of rotten paper. There were comb marks in the wet filth around the yard where someone had been brushing it all together. Anzani paused and regarded it. A bad stink, eh? It better not go through my shop or we sue the fucking Council, eh? He shook his head and looked up at the sky in disgust. More rain tomorrow too, so that's great, eh? More shit for my yard. He handed me the clipboard, map and keys and I splashed over to the van.

Anzani picked his way to the gates and swung them open, looking pained at having to tread his good shoes all over the yard, seeming suddenly much older under the rain. As I edged the van out he kept glancing down at his feet and at the wheels rolling past the toes.

I don't know what made me drive to the library first. Some intuition, or morbid fear. And she was there, waiting, hooded in a short dark anorak, not at all surprised to see the slow white van make its way toward her and stop, the damp engine rattling. As I leaned across the cab to open the lock on the door I felt a strong, almost suffocating sense of time suddenly folding, or closing like the lid of a box, over every small action now – my fingers on the plastic latch, my foot on the pedal of the brake – sealing me in to a place with no clear way back to the outside world I was leaving.

I'm cold, she said. I've been waiting. Can you put the heating on?

I didn't ask her where she'd left her suitcase, or where she was staying now – it didn't seem relevant somehow – and she didn't offer any information.

I drove for what seemed like a long, unbroken time along winding country roads that seemed to repeat themselves, mile on nearsighted mile, through endless curtains of rain. At a crossroads I saw the black and white sign for Strata Florida, Ystrad Fflur, and remembered the misericords at Clarach, spirited from the abbey there when it was left to wrack and ruin. It seemed like whole seasons and years had passed since that walk along the cliff path in the sun.

At one point I reached over and rested my hand on her thigh, but Christine didn't respond except to glance at it briefly as if to see what unexpected weight had settled on her leg. I left it lying there a while, then lifted it back to the wheel.

The road to the last cafe wasn't much more than a farm track and Christine tensed each time we thumped in and out of the potholes that littered it. They were filled with brown water and it was impossible to tell the shallow puddles from bone-jarring craters. In the end I slowed the van right down and tried to weave through, though the slow, clumsy swaying of the van kept Christine just as rigid in her seat as when we were crunching into them.

There were toilets beside the cafe – a couple of weathered Portacabins on stilts, the doors pegged open – and as soon as I'd brought the van to a standstill Christine let herself out and strode through the rain to the wooden steps of the Ladies. I watched her go in through the open doorway and caught a glimpse of her reflection in a mirror as she rounded a partition to get to the stalls.

I dealt with the small delivery, signing over a few crates of soft drinks and biscuits, and was surprised to see that Christine still hadn't returned to the van when I got back. After a minute or so of silence a carload of what looked like students pulled up alongside and one of them, the young guy driving, jumped out to sprint to the Gents. He held his arms over his head and shook it wildly as he ran the few yards to the hut, as if astonished by the rain. While he was gone the others in the car – another lad and two girls – started clowning with the horn and in a moment he came grinning to the door of the hut, holding his cock in one hand, like an angler showing off a limp, pink fish, and giving them the finger with the other. They cheered and he went back in to finish while one of them jabbed even harder on the horn, all three cat-calling out of the opened windows. One of the girls caught my eye as she yelled and I looked away to the ruins of what must have been a barn when the cafe was still a farmhouse – a low grey wall and in the middle of it the remains of its wide entrance, the tall archway intact but all of it roofless now under the rain.

The car was gone by the time Christine came out and down the steps of her hut. I leaned across to open the door for her.

What was all that? she asked, her voice taut, as if I were somehow to blame.

Just kids messing around. Drunk, I think. They've gone now. I took a good look at her. She was less pale than when we'd left town but her face still looked drawn and tired.

It made me afraid to come out, she said. I didn't know what was happening. She sat back, staring at the dark sacks of cloud heaped above the Portacabins and the tumbledown barn.

That's the last delivery, I said. It's getting late. We'd better head back.

She lolled her head from side to side against the back of the seat. Not yet, she said. You could take us somewhere.

Where?

I don't know. Only if you want to. She was speaking so low I could hardly hear her over the drumming rain. I leaned closer. You could drive somewhere quiet, she said.

I nodded, feeling my mouth become dry.

It was a struggle to restart the engine and for a moment I imagined us stranded there, and all the strangeness of the day – and the days before it – ending in nothing more than a kind of mechanical farce of phone calls, frustrations, and a tow-truck hauling us back to reality. But finally the ignition caught and I rolled the van out of the car park and along the narrow track to the main junction.

Where now? I said.

Not back to town. Turn left and see where it goes.

It goes to the farm, I said, if we turn off again higher up.

She nodded as if she already knew and soon we were in the midst of familiar forested hills I'd only ever climbed alone before, and on foot.

It's along there, I said, slowing the van to a crawl. Away to our left the farm's dirt track branched off through a clump of spindly firs, its red mud and bare stones unchanged in the two years since I'd last trudged over them. The road itself widened opposite the turning – a muddy, tyre-rutted lay-by where trailers were sometimes unhooked and left between loads. It was empty now. I bumped the van into the space, leaving the road clear. We can turn here, I said. The rain had eased as we wound higher across the face of the hill and just a few heavy drops broke the silence at intervals, blown from the overhanging branches, maybe.

Let's go out and get some air, she said, unclipping her seat belt. I saw a path going down into the trees a little way back. I'd like to see where it goes. She opened her door and slipped out.

I didn't want to cut the engine again but had no choice now. I turned the key and joined her where she stood peering downhill through the ranks of trees.

Let's go back to it, she said, and skirted the muddy clearing to reach the gravelled road.

We tramped downhill for a hundred yards or so until the spider's leg of the trail appeared. I recognised it, and had even wandered along it once not long after I'd arrived to work at the farm, but didn't say anything to her. It must have been a Forestry Commission access track at some point, maybe when the hill was planted, but now it was just a grassed-over green way amongst the pines. Christine strode on ahead of me, startling a few sheep and lambs grazing in the margin of the trees. They skittered past her, then saw me and turned again, confused, the lambs bleating. In the end they waited watchfully for us to pass. Not one of them pushed through deeper into the branches.

I can see buildings, Christine said. She'd stopped walking where the path seemed to have ended in a broad clearing. I caught up with her and looked into the trees further down the slope and to the left where she was pointing. Beyond a screen of young pines a low, broken-down wall was visible, and behind it a handful of structures built from the same pale, roughly shaped stone. She started toward them and I followed automatically.

It must have been a village, she said. So many ruins all around. If I had to live anywhere I'd like to live in a place like this.

They're all over the hill, I said, wondering what she meant. Old farms from before the forestry.

Is that all they are?

I laughed despite myself. What else could they be? All the way up here?

She shrugged. Here's the rain again, she said, and moved close to me under the branches.

We stood in the gloom of the pines for some time, watching the cloud burst leap up from the stones and batter the dense clumps of nettles in the old doorways. She rested her head against my arm as the minutes dragged on and the rain gradually eased.

How long can we wait? she asked at last, and slipped

her arm under my jacket and around my waist. It's getting dark already.

It's just the clouds and the trees making it dark, I said, not wanting to move now she was close again. It's not late.

She pressed more tightly and I realised she was shivering. Check the time, she said.

I lifted my arm to read my watch. Nearly five, I told her, though she could see for herself.

Show me the farm before we go.

I started up the slope, leading this time, careful not to whip any of the trailing branches back at Christine. Our feet were almost silent on the brown carpet of needles and any sounds we did make were masked by the rain's long soughing all around us. More than once I found myself stopping just to check there was still someone behind me, and each time Christine halted when I looked, keeping a certain distance between us, staring back without expression until I turned and trudged on again.

We'd climbed the main part of the slope and the white of the van was visible through the trees when Christine caught up with me and said quietly that a ram was watching us from the path. Look how it's staring, she said. He must have followed us up.

Move a bit deeper into the trees, I said, and she laughed. I'd been butted by the old ram on Pugh's farm a couple of times – losing my feet completely once – and I knew that given a good run up a full-grown ram could snap a leg or a hip without much trouble. Go on, I insisted. Move further in.

She stooped low and eased her way through the next rank of trees and the ram lowered its head, sizing us up. Fuck off! Get away! I yelled at it, and Christine laughed again. The ram stayed completely still, letting the downpour wash over it, the heavy drops soaking into the dirty wool of its coat or spattering on its bowed, bony head. It's all right, she said. He's just curious, like us. She smoothed her hair back with the flat of her hand, then carried on up to the van.

I turned and followed her, glancing back once to see the ram still motionless but staring after me through the rain.

Christine stayed ahead of me until she reached the road, then waited under what little cover there was below the pines' wiry branches while I crossed the track and opened up the cab. We can't walk in this, I called to her, it's hopeless. I'll drive on a bit and you can see the farm from higher up.

Every few hundred yards there were passing places for farm traffic and as we climbed higher it wasn't long before I found one that overlooked the farm nested in trees in the distance. Only the roofs of the main building and tallest sheds were visible, but beyond them we could see the fields and dry-stone walls with their sprinkling of distant sheep. I left the engine running while Christine craned forward and rubbed the mist from the windscreen, trying to make sense of the view. The rain had stopped again and the far side of the valley was visible, its tops shrouded in folds of dark cloud. They were drifting towards us like smoke, heavy and grainy in the late light, blowing inland from the sea. Where's the caravan? she asked.

Somewhere in the trees. Not far from the roof of the barn.

I wish we could see it, she said.

Why?

She didn't answer.

A small dark figure was following the line of the highest wall, where the last of the pasture gave way to the bracken and heather of the hilltops. Meirion, I said. Look. I pointed out the tramping figure, inching distantly along the pale contour of the stonework. We watched until he reached the edge of the pine plantation above the farmhouse, then lost sight of him as he crossed a ditch with its black thread of water and passed into the trees. A fine drizzle began, noiseless, speckling the windscreen and blotting out the brief glimpse of the fields.

I heard the snick of Christine's seat belt opening, heard her body in its nylon rain jacket sliding from her seat, then felt the movement of her hands on my thighs, the tugging of her fingers at the button and zip of my jeans. I looked down at the dark wet strands of her hair, tied back tight to the scalp, and with a feeling more like sadness than desire smelt the resinous, wintry scent of the woods and the weather that had closed in all around us rising up from her bowed head. And then the world and everything in it closed down to a single point of soft, smooth warmth as her mouth closed over me and moved in a slow, mesmeric rhythm that carried me, gently, body and mind, like the dipping and rising of the sea. I remembered the sensation I'd felt alone on the small waves, under the stars, the night I followed Christine and swam out from the cliffs. I was suspended again now, aware that my whole life was swaying on a single, dizzying, balancing point, fine as the tip of a nerve. Why didn't I wake and move, shout out even? Why didn't I struggle back to solid land – to Jenny, Michael, a life of choices like solid objects that might be built up, with luck and time, into the same shapes other people made of their lives? I'd swum back to shore that night with Christine, and kept my skin. Why couldn't I swim back now? Was it simply and brutally that I didn't know I could be loved?

The sound of a sluggish engine, and of big wheels bumping down the dirt road, came down to us from somewhere beyond the bend where we'd parked. I felt Christine's body tense and freeze under my arm, and abruptly she pulled away and lifted herself to sit upright in her seat. We both watched the truck drawing near through the bad light. It came down the incline slowly, lurching from rut to rut. The driver, a pale narrow-faced man in a farmer's flat cap, stared at us – at Christine in particular – as he passed but didn't alter his fixed, bored expression. In the back of the flat-bed truck stood a heifer wrapped tight to the neck in heavy, clear polythene. It seemed to be lashed to the side panels with canvas straps. Look at that, Christine murmured. It's awful. Why is it wrapped up like that?

We should get back, I said at last, once the truck was out of sight.

Don't go fast. Don't catch up with the truck, Christine said. She shifted nearer the door and stared out towards the farm, still hidden behind mist and rain, then reached up and dragged the seat belt across her chest.

At the outskirts of town I asked Christine where she wanted to be dropped. Have you got anywhere to stay? I asked.

Drop me at the station. I left my bags in the lockers there.

But where are you staying? Have you got anywhere to

sleep?

It's fine, she said. Just drop me at the station.

The only parking space I could find was outside Jenny's old digs – at any moment I half expected to see Mrs Horace dragging her tartan shopping trolley along the pavement towards us – but the road stayed empty except for the occasional car hissing through puddles of water, their bleary headlights staring through the gloom.

She opened the door and would have slipped down to the pavement and away without a word, I'm sure, so I said: Chris. Will I see you again?

I don't know. Will you? she said, then stepped down and slammed the door without looking back.

The lights were still on in the shop-front window when I parked at Anzani's, though the closed sign was up. He must have been listening for the engine because I'd hardly finished locking the van when he opened the door behind me, the shop bell tinkling festively at his back.

Hey Luke, what weather, eh? Everything go okay?

Fine.

The rain held you up, eh? Any problems with the engine.

I gave him the keys. Some, I said, but I got it going again. Just the damp.

It's a bastard in the wet, he said, nodding. He took the keys and that's when we both noticed Christine watching us from across the street. She hadn't collected her bags yet and I couldn't tell if she was surprised to see us or had cut through from the station with every intention of following. She gave no sign that she knew me. He stared back at her for a second, then looked at me again and cleared his throat. I'll take it round to the yard. He glanced once more at Christine and frowned as if trying to place her. You get home now, he said, and retreated back into the shop.

*

Jenny reacted better than I'd expected to my getting in so late. Whatever she'd felt and thought throughout the day while I was gone, now she wore the same calm, almost business-like mask that she'd put on earlier that morning to wake me and re-launch our lives.

I made a casserole, she said, helping me peel off my soaked jacket and hanging it, dripping, from the back of the door. Change into dry clothes and I'll fetch it down from the kitchen. Were the roads ok? I was getting worried about you.

I had to go out to Strata Florida. Then out near the farm. The van cut out for a while, too. It was just really slow going, with all the rain on those crappy roads. I'm so tired, I said, and meant it – I felt as if I could drop to the floor and sleep.

You must be hungry, too, she said. I nodded, forcing a smile, though it seemed impossible to even imagine eating. My empty stomach felt closed tight on itself, hard as a fist.

I asked Mrs Clement to take Michael for a few hours, so we could eat in peace, just the two of us. I said I'd collect him at ten, before they go to bed. She's good to us, isn't she?

She is, I said.

While Jenny prepared the food upstairs in the kitchen I changed out of my wet clothes and then stared out of the bedroom window to the road below and the sea. The prom was almost empty – just a few walkers struggling against the wind, hunching against the rain and the spray lashing up from the seawall. It was almost dark now, hours early, the evening sun completely blotted out by the low, black storm-clouds rolling in without a break from the west. When I heard the table being set I went through to the living room.

Jenny had laid out the table with a cloth and wine glasses and was trying to fix a candle onto a cheap brass holder I didn't recognise. She smiled distractedly at me and tried again to get the candle secured. There's a little spike in here to hold the candle, but the wax just keeps crumbling, she said.

Where did you find that?

In the basement kitchen, in one of the cupboards. I was looking for nice things, like serviette rings and side plates. I thought we never have anything like that, and it would be nice just for once. I found the candle there, too, but I think it's too old. It's all dried up and crumbly. She sighed. I'll light it and make a pool of wax, and stick it in that. Will that work, do you think?

I'll try it, I said.

I just want it to be nice.

Jenny had bought two bottles of wine and we both drank steadily through the meal, each of us afraid to talk, I think. Somehow I managed to clear my plate though the food seemed to sit in my stomach like rocks. I cleared the dishes, made my way, drunk and numb, up to the kitchen with them and left them to soak. In the next door bathroom I doused my face with cold water before leaning out of the open window for a while, fighting back the urge to throw up into the toilet. Even at the back of the building the wind had tipped the bins in the yard and was clattering through the rubbish, rolling cans and bottles over the concrete. There was no sign of the dog. When my head began to clear I went back down to Jenny.

She was sitting cross-legged on the sofa, smoking a long skinny joint. Drew gave me some, she said, smiling slackly. I thought what the hell, we need to relax tonight. She took another draw and held it out to me, but I shook my head. She hadn't smoked since falling pregnant and the sight and smell of it now seemed ominous in some way.

What if the Clements smell it? They'll go nuts, I said.

She nodded. Open the window, she said.

Outside, the waves were beating at the topmost stones of the sea wall, plumes of spray snaking up as high as the window, wetting my face with their cold and salt. Through the soles of my feet I could feel the fabric of the building quiver with each heavy, booming crash. After a while I realised Jenny had come to stand and watch beside me. She stubbed the joint on the outside sill and flicked the butt out to the side of the window. It whirled up and disappeared. Close the window, she said, everything's getting blown about in here.

I took a last look at the breakers rolling in from the bay: black beyond the glimmer of the streetlights, streaked with foam. Beyond a certain point they were invisible in the dark, looming into view almost fully formed, and it made them seem unnatural, almost alien, as if they were sweeping in not from the familiar waters of the bay, but directly from the blackness of space.

Jenny was in the bedroom when I left the window to join her. I waited, sitting back on the sofa with my eyes closed, wishing the whole churn of the evening were done and I could hide myself in sleep. If I could have slipped into death then, quietly, by a simple effort of will, I would have. But I felt her weight settling into the cushion at my side, and I opened my eyes again. She'd brought through a plastic shopping bag and set it down between us.

Christine left this, she said, frowning at the bag as if opening it and looking inside were a puzzle too hard for her to solve.

Do you know what's in it?

Shopping. Little things she bought when we were out together. Before we quarrelled.

We should send them on. Did she forget them?

No. She left a note with it. It said she didn't want any of it and was leaving it for us, for letting her stay. I don't want any of it, but I thought I should let you see it first, if you want. Unless you want to keep anything I'll take it down to the bins when I go to fetch Michael.

Did the note say anything else?

Jenny didn't reply at first, then: Yes. But it was written to me, she said.

I took the bag and gently shook the contents out onto the sofa. There were a few small presents for Michael: a knitted cotton cap, a baby-sized T-shirt with a star on it and Twinkle Twinkle embroidered underneath, and a loosely stuffed monkey, the outsize label still hanging on a plastic staple through its ear. It was beige with skewed limbs and had a serious, melancholic set to its face, and I thought I could imagine Christine being taken with it. Next to it was an A4 sized poster, furled into a scroll. I ran the rubber band off it and opened it out. I'd seen the picture before in cheap poster shops and on students' walls at parties –

white gulls flying over a blue sea and a quote from Plato – 'They can because they think they can.'

Jenny made a soft, catching sound in her throat and I thought she was about to laugh at the poster, but when I looked up she was crying.

Jen, what's wrong? I said.

She shook her head and bit hard on a knuckle, as if to stop herself howling, her eyes screwed tight in a kind of torment and her whole body quaking. I let the poster spring back on itself and put it back in the bag.

What is it? I said, frightened now. She rarely cried – had cried properly and bitterly just once or twice in all the time I knew her – and this was worse than tears: it was like she was struggling to hold back some sudden, wild grief, or some physical agony. For Christ's sake, Jen, just tell me. Please. What's wrong?

I waited then – five long minutes or more – until she brought herself under control again and began to breathe more normally. That poster made me think of something, she said. It's something I've got to tell you. But I can't tell you now – I've drunk too much. I'll just go to pieces again. I'll tell you one day, I promise. When we've forgotten all about the last two weeks.

I reached for her clenched hand and drew it away from her mouth, then held it in my lap.

It's not about us, she said. It's about me. You don't need to worry.

Of course I'm worried. Just tell me, I said. It'll be ok.

She pushed herself upright from the sofa and walked unsteadily to the table. Taking one of the paper napkins she blew her nose loudly and then folded the tissue into a wad and dabbed at her eyes. I'll tell you about the poster anyway, she said. That's just a silly story. It's not what made me cry. She took a deep breath. When I was good friends with Bill we used to smoke dope and watch lots of cartoons on his video player, you know? Over and over again. Whole afternoons. We were such stoners. She smiled sheepishly, pressing the tissue to her nose. And anyway, one of his flatmates had that poster up on the wall, and we used to make fun of it and make up other tag lines like 'They can because they're fucking seagulls for Christ's sake', and whenever Wile E. Coyote ran off a cliff after Bugs Bunny, and you know how he never falls until he realizes he's in mid-air, and then he goes – gulp! – and whoosh, he has to fall? Well Bill would point at the poster and say, See – Plato's right! She laughed and bubbled her nose into the tissue before coming back to sit with me again. He had this whole stupid theory about how cartoons reflect the way our minds actually work – so they're like pictures of how we really feel about reality, even though we know logically that they don't match up to the facts. And that's what makes them comforting, you know, and funny. When he's stoned, Bill can really go off on one.

I wanted to hold her, then, but couldn't bring myself to. Jenny picked up the gangly monkey and set it between her knees. I won't throw you out, she said to it, you ugly little sad thing. I'll take you to a charity shop. She began collecting up the other bits and pieces, dropping them back into the bag. I'll get rid of these and fetch Michael, she said.

Eleven

A solitary green-keeper standing way off on one of the higher tees watches me jogging across the wide ninth fairway, leaving the warehouse behind me for the very last time, though I've no way of knowing it yet. He stares after me a while but soon I'm in the rough, heading for the trees along the river and the public footpath there. The long grass between the trees soaks my boots and jeans right up to the knees and the wet, flapping denim sticks to my shins as I walk.

The river when I get to it is still rising, bullying over long wads of drowned grass. I cross at a new steel footbridge floored with grilled panels and through the mesh walkway I can see the river's heavy, brown swirls nearly lapping my soles.

Near the harbour, where the river widens and shallows for its last few hundred yards before emptying into the bay, I start passing fishermen hurrying to find places after their day's work in offices, shops, schools. One or two are already thigh-deep in the currents, their lines licking out onto the eddies and sweeping down. A heavy fish leaps mid-stream and one of the fishermen rolls a swift, graceful cast out to cover it.

Duw, they're running now, eh? the fisherman calls to another much older angler just down from him. Really running, by Christ. He strips the line in expertly, working it fast to begin with, then slower over likely lies. Before going on I wait for him to lay his line out again, hearing the heavy lure fizz across the path ahead of me on each back-cast.

Just before I reach the harbour one of the men hooks into a strong fish that doesn't show itself at first but just ploughs deep downstream for the open bay. The man's dressed more casually than the others – in denims and hiking boots, maybe he'd rushed to get to his spot on the river – and because he can't wade deep it takes him a good five minutes to get the fight under control. Without a net, he tries to haul the fish into a shallow backwater where he can drop the rod and lay his hands on it. Twice he gets it on its flank in the back-eddy, and each time it spasms out into the flow again before he can make his move. On the third attempt it thrashes the wrong way and hurls itself against the steep bank where, after a stunned moment, it starts to pound the mud wall with its tail. The sound of it carries far enough upstream for some of the other fishermen to crane their necks and stare. The man in the denim jacket splashes down onto his knees to it, blocking my view. I see his arm rise and fall as he bludgeons it with a rock. It makes the same sound the fish made, beating its tail against the bank.

Just past the mouth of the river I stop and watch the cormorants by the pier, thinking of the morning and of Jenny's dream. It seems years since I woke; years since I stood in the bathroom hearing Clement's dog barking in the yard below. One of the birds lifts its dark wings, as if ready to pronounce a benediction.

As I pass the penny arcade at the front of the pier the swing doors sweep open, nearly knocking me back, and a gang of school boys, still in uniform, push each other out onto the prom, laughing and elbowing. Did you fucking see me, though? one of them keeps asking the others in a high, piping voice. They ignore him. The dummy fortune-teller in its glass booth jolts into life and starts going through its routine: the painted gypsy head jerking back, the wooden hand juddering over the crystal ball and a loud robotic voice promising *All the fun of the future, all the fun of the future – inside!* I follow the school kids along the road for a short while then turn left down the bay while they jostle and bicker straight on into town.

Inside the entrance hall to Bethesda I can hear the Clements' piano being played – first a few bars from some piano concerto, then *Greensleeves*. I stop to knock at the door and collect Michael, but on impulse decide to leave it for a while and give myself some time alone before taking him off their hands. For once there'd been no sign of Mrs Clement at the bay window. I move quickly up the first flight of stairs to get out of sight of the hall. On the second floor I pass the lanky, ginger-haired student on his way to the bath. He's naked except for an off-white towel pinched round his waist and a pair of earphones trailing to the Walkman in his hand. He grins and I slip past him before he can speak. When I get to the apartment door I lean my forehead against it, hearing the blood knocking in my temples as I dig in my pocket for the keys.

At first Christine doesn't turn from the cot to face me. She waits, drinking in my surprise and silence, then, still keeping her back to me, says, I thought you'd be home. I came to find you, and you weren't here.

Jesus, Chris. How did you get in?

The landlord saw me on the stairs. He said they were

looking after Michael, so I took him and came here.

You took Michael?

Now she turns, but doesn't leave the cot. You knew I'd come back. You knew I hadn't left.

I nod dumbly. She's wearing the same clothes she wore the afternoon she arrived: the collarless, cream blouse buttoned to the throat and the simple, pale blue skirt like a patch of sky. My heart's knocking in my throat and I have to pause before trusting myself to speak. How long have you been here?

She shrugs. I don't know, she says. Maybe an hour. Maybe two. When is Jennifer coming back?

Not till late. She has to make up for the time she took off last week.

Good. She runs a hand over her hair, but doesn't come towards me.

When I step inside I see that the bedroom door is wide open. There are cardboard boxes sitting on the bed: some of the boxes we'd stowed away for storage when we moved in. She's emptied them out, I realise as I look more closely: the bed is covered with photographs, letters and documents – my driver's license, even our birth certificates – unfolded and laid out amongst the jumble of images. When I turn to her, speechless, I notice that the cot is littered with them too: old photographs of my own and Jenny's, spread over Michael's blankets and even taped to the wooden bars, walling him in.

I found them in your box-room; I was nosy, is all she says, and all I can do is shake my head and stare at the strange, random collage.

Most of the photographs are Jenny's – one of the two girls, her and Christine, sat on an almost empty, monochrome beach; a couple of Jenny alone with a black cat half the size of herself. Some of their mother, alone or with the girls. Some of their father, as a young man – one of him cloaked in graduation robes – and I realise with a start that Christine has added photographs of her own that she must have brought with her. I start gathering them up.

Not yet. Please. Leave them a bit longer. I don't believe in photographs, she adds flatly, but I wanted to see everything all at once.

I nod, too bewildered to ask or care much what she means, and catch sight of a photograph of myself, as a small boy with my father. I'm sitting on a low red-brick wall, my father stood to my left in a dark security guard's uniform – just one of his many short-lived jobs as I was growing up – arms folded stoutly. We're in bright sunshine and both squinting so hard our eyes are completely hidden.

You're not glad to see me. You're frightened. I knew you would be.

I shake my head, still lost for words and distracted by the photograph. To the right of the wall there's just a glimpse of the red and white chevrons marking some kind of security barrier. I have a sudden, sharp memory of balancing my body on it as my father moves it up and down for me, an improvised swing: the ground falling away from my feet and then the ride back to earth, as slowly as falling in a dream.

Why won't you come near me then?

I lay the photographs back down on the bed and move to the cot, each movement feeling separate and awkward. Is Michael sleeping?

Yes, she says, moving to block my view. Don't disturb

him. Her head tilts to one side and her eyelids almost close, as if a sudden drowsiness is washing over her, too. He's peaceful, she says. She takes my hand and steers me to the sofa. The door to the box-room is ajar and through the gap I can see the mess she's made of my books, files and papers.

Don't watch me, she instructs, and turns away to unbutton her blouse.

Chris, I don't know, I say, but still with her back to me she slips off her skirt and underwear, then curls her body foetus-like on the sofa.

Hold me, she says, inching her body forward to make room for my body behind her.

I lower myself on to the cushions and her knees straighten a little to make room, though her arms stay folded across her chest.

For some time we just stay like that, listening to each other's breathing and feeling the beating of each other's heart. Eventually the sound comes of footsteps on the stairs and Alex's door opens, then bangs shut. Soon the sound of his music begins to leak through the wall, a looping dance beat. His door opens and slams shut again as he heads upstairs to the kitchen or bathroom.

You can't love anyone, can you? she murmurs.

I start to reply, but stop myself before making a sound.

She reaches down to find my hand where it rests on her hip and guides it between her thighs, opening them enough to let me in before closing them again and trapping me there.

Without moving my head I can see a top corner of the window and the grey wastes of sky beyond. Every time the wind gusts a few drops of rain tap at the glass and the old sash window rattles in its wooden frame.

Put your fingers inside me.

She eases her legs apart again, just enough, and I do what she says, surprised at her wetness. I feel myself growing hard, despite myself.

Deeper.

Alex thumps down the stairs to his room again. The music dies and in its place comes the sound of his television. Voices fencing back and forth.

You're like me, she says finally, whispering. We should have been born with gills. She shivers and I rest my forehead against the back of her skull, breathe in the fragrance from the salty oils of her scalp.

Jennifer won't want to live like this for much longer. She won't stay with you. You know that, don't you? Michael is all that matters to her now.

I close my eyes and remember again swimming after her into the bay at night. Turning my cold, bare body to look back at the world, floating clear of it, unable to fall.

I was like a wife and a mother to my father, she says. I was everything to him, in the end. She presses her body harder against mine, as if for warmth, and shivers again. Jennifer was pregnant by that man, Bill Kerrigan, she says then, and he talked her into an abortion, not long before she met you. She'll go back to him, I think, now she's got Michael and feels like she can forgive him. Or someone like him. Someone from the real world.

I don't ask her how she knows. Some confession in a cafe, maybe, or some drunken heart-to-heart on one of the nights when I left them in the living room and tried to sleep through their low, muddled babble with Michael in the cot at my side. Yes – a night like that, I think, and I remember Jenny, the evening after Christine left, crying so bitterly, recalling those afternoons with Kerrigan, the father of her first child. It's not about us, she'd said. You don't have to worry.

I lift my head clear of Christine's dark, sleek hair and look down along the length of her body. Her limbs, stiff and blueish, seem shadowless and flattened, more like engravings than flesh in the iron light.

It's night when Jenny finally twists her key in the lock and pushes open the door to the apartment. She stands a little while on the threshold, in the dark, maybe sensing all the heartbreak and trouble that will flood in on all of us, unstoppably, with the simple lighting of the room.

Luke? she calls. Luke? Then silence while her hand finds the switch, and silence while she stands confused in the bulb's glare, noticing the photographs first, maybe, and Michael, still sleeping, his deep, deep sleep, lying motionless amongst them.

Twelve

The years make Russian dolls of our lives, nesting one self inside the other, a neat, coffined family of near identical forms – habits, needs, errors – that get heavier with the decades, more full of rattling ghosts. Inside we go, one self after the other, and each one forever; and if we could make out anything in there, where no light gets through, it would be the contours of our own head in front of our face.

I like to think it was by accident that Christine stepped in front of a rush-hour bus, just weeks after returning to the house her father left her. But I did discover, much later, that she'd tried to commit suicide, three days after her father's funeral, with the same sleeping pills she would use to make Michael sleep so deeply – almost too deep to ever come back, and maybe he never came back the same child – that long, grey August afternoon. But if she tried to die a second time, she failed, and lingered on for years, trapped in God knows what kind of limbo. Jenny and her mother refused to the bitter end to let the hospital turn off the machinery around her hospital bed. It was the only way they had to punish her, perhaps. Five years of that, before she managed to let go, sinking down to whatever currents carry us off into the dark.

While Christine drifted alone inside her head, or more probably far beyond it, I made my way to France, Spain and Morocco, scratching a living on farms, vineyards and camp-sites as I went. By my second year of wandering I'd made enough contacts in the loose, almost casual small-time underworld of drifting pickpockets, petty dealers and tobacco smugglers to get better paid work – and as much solitude as I needed – tramping across the border with rucksacks full of contraband cigarettes, sometimes bricks of Moroccan hash. Occasionally I'd come across British newspapers left lying on benches or on the breakfast tables of cheap hostels, and it amused me vaguely to realise that my life had become some small flaking off of that long Thatcherite dream: self-sufficient, entrepreneurial, a busy little insect in the service of free trade. I used the network of pilgrim trails around the Baztan valley in the Basque country, wore a scallop shell in my cap, and was robbed occasionally, nearly murdered once on the banks of a small stream, but never caught.

I slept more soundly in the hills, barns and pilgrim shelters along the Camino than in any of the other places I've known since leaving Bethesda, though even after long, exhausting days of hiking I often woke before daylight with Christine's white face floating in my mind, or Michael's.

I came back once before she died, for my grandfather's Baptist funeral under a daylong veil of soft valleys rain, and took the chance to visit her in the sterile little hospital cell that Jenny and her mother had condemned her to. I was surprised to learn from one of the nurses that she was visited every other day by her sister, who would speak to her at length, in private, as soon as she was left alone. I sat with her for a little time, the nurse in attendance, as she was obliged to be for a stranger, but couldn't find anything to say. As I left, I explained that I didn't want Jenny knowing about my visit. I won't be back, I said, so she doesn't need to know. It would just upset her. The nurse looked at me quizzically, but shrugged and said, all right then, if you think so. But if she ever checks the visitors' log she'll be able to see for herself. I can't change that for you.

No, I said. I understand, and smiled to reassure her, though if I could have paid every penny I owned to cover my traces, I would have. And I've often wondered since whether she kept her word, or if my saying goodbye to Christine became one last hurt I inflicted on Jenny before slipping like an assassin out of her life completely.

By the time of my grandmother's funeral, soon after, in bright March sunshine, Christine was gone too. Her ashes, I discovered later, were scattered by Jenny and her mother in the Irish Sea she'd so often swum in. So maybe there was some forgiveness, some kind of peace made, in the end.

I was in my thirties before I came back to Britain. I had money in the bank from a thousand illicit border-crossings, and I rented a tiny flat in the great anonymity of London. I went back to studying and was amazed to find that the work I'd completed so many years before still counted for something, though I didn't have the heart to go back to any of the subjects I'd thought about and written on in that small box-room at Bethesda. In fact, I changed my name and studied theology, and after graduation applied for a part-time doctorate in early Church doctrine and history, back in Wales, at a college whose windows faced the sea again. My thesis, along with my research, wanders on its way as obscurely as I once did; I have no intention of ever finishing it.

I've no faith of any kind in God, and I know that my compulsion to devote so much of my thinking to religion must be, at bottom, a simple longing for the father I lost, and expiation for the missing father I so quickly became in my turn, though I feel no embarrassment about that need. And I wonder, too, if all my tracking down of God through his big, empty lair is a means of finding some way back to Jenny and Christine; a sense that there might be a thread left behind in the labyrinth where their father lurked, some human trace, lying all these years in the dark. Am I really like him, that half-mad, controlling, hypocrite believer, as Jenny claimed all those years ago? It's possible she was right, I suppose: who else ever knew me? Is that why Christine – lost in her own private maze – tried to break through its walls?

But it's hopeless, I know, to think in these kinds of ways. It's like trying to read the shapes of shadows in a cave by flooding it with light. It comes from being too much alone, for much too long.

Now, if I believe anything that can be put into words, it's that there's a kind of solidarity in the enormous, continuous effort the mind must make to see meaning in the world – to go on living, to keep the spirit alive in its shell – and the vast, impersonal energies that bind the atoms at their nuclear hearts. I imagine the universe, which is nothing if it isn't one great idea, the one great archetype of thought, working hard to believe in itself, in the face of entropy and all its billion cooling stars. I think it's tired, and can't rest.

There are two small Methodist chapels within walking distance of the cottage I rent – Hebron and Salem, one originally Calvinist, the other Wesleyan – perched on either side of the southernmost tip of Pembrokeshire, and they're subject to entropy too, of course, lapsing into ruin one loose slate and one burst water pipe at a time. I like to attend one or other of their services most Sundays, watching and listening from a seat just inside the door, enjoying the faintly sung hymns, the mild, encouraging sermons, the bowed backs of the old people's heads at prayer, the whisper and smell of rain from the sea, crossing the wet fields outside. The chapels have to share a minister between them, now – the Reverend Carys Bethell – a young, humorous, intelligent woman more likely to quote poetry, Karl Barth and philosophy than the Old Testament. The congregations are a pitiful contrast to her energies, of course: three or four of the faithful in each, fading away almost symbiotically with the rotting buildings they come to worship in. I don't know what the elders in such a time-bound, traditional place made of being preached to by a young woman when she first arrived. But that atmosphere of timelessness operates both ways I suppose, and sometimes I wonder if they've even noticed yet. Is she slowly winning them round to some notion of a gentler, much more human God than the builders of these chapels would ever have recognised or even wanted? Or is she simply outlasting their frowns and gossip for a while, like the tallest candle in a power-cut?

She's curious about me, it's clear, and often meets my eye in the midst of a service, though I make sure to slip away before she can keep me in conversation. I did stay a little longer once, to thank her after a sermon had both puzzled and moved me. She'd taken a poem as her text – one of the lyrics in the voice of God in Rilke's *Book of Hours*. 'Nearby is the country they call life,' she read, leaning forward eagerly, as she often does, as if she might one day launch herself from the tall oak pulpit. 'You will know it by its seriousness.'

The words reminded me, though I couldn't say exactly why, of a scene in a film I'd watched once – something French – in a small art-house cinema during my time in London. I used to go there for the weekday matinees, knowing it would be almost deserted then, and would sometimes drift into sleep or lose myself in memories amongst the rows of empty seats. In the film there was a trial scene where the judge shouted out his charges and questions at a line of cowed prisoners. Then, because the prisoners' belts had been confiscated in their cells, one of the men finds his trousers falling down, and is terrified. For an awful moment there's nothing but silence. Then the judge begins to laugh. And soon the entire court – and the humiliated prisoner – is laughing helplessly too.

Helpless – that was the thing. I remember standing and groping my way out of the cinema without watching the rest of the film. The day was bright and hot outside; dusty and roaring with mid-day traffic. It must have been deep into summer. I walked to a nearby park and sat on a bench until my heart stopped racing.

I waited for her when the service ended, outside the porch, smoking a cigarette in the watery sun, nodding at the few old widows and widowers as they left. They each seemed a little startled to see me loitering in the brightness there.

Oh. Hello, she said, when she finally appeared. I see you at the back there most Sundays, don't I? But you never stay for introductions. She turned away briefly to lock the door, then faced me again with steady, pale green eyes and a bright, frank smile that seemed, in the friendliest of ways, to demand I explain myself.

I quoted the lines of poetry to her. You spoke so well about most of the poem, I told her, smiling. But I was sitting there hoping you'd explain what those particular lines meant, and you didn't. I can't get them out of my head, and I've no idea why.

Explain! she said, laughing. I'm a woman of the cloth. It wouldn't be right for me to do anything as wicked as that to a poem.

I laughed with her, and we shook hands and introduced ourselves a little shyly.

I'm sorry, but I'm always here under false pretences, I told her. I'm not a believer. Not even agnostic. I just find it restful to listen to it all.

She nodded decisively. I think that's as good a reason as any for being here, she said. To be honest, you always look so gloomy in the shadows, I was thinking you must be some disapproving old diehard building up evidence for a quarrel. I get my fair share.

Maybe you'll convert me and I'll become one.

She laughed again, and I longed suddenly to find an excuse to keep her talking, but couldn't think of anything beyond some clumsy, rushed invitation that would surely unnerve her, and the impulse passed as quickly as it had come. Well, listen, she said. I'm so glad we've spoken at last, but I must get going.

Yes, I said. Of course.

Honestly, I'm sorry – I'd love to talk. But I've an afternoon service in one the old folks' homes in town today. Next week, maybe? She stepped lightly across the gravel toward her small blue car, pausing after opening its door to grin over her shoulder and wave. I watched her drive off and listened for the engine fading into silence before starting on the walk home.

Soon enough, I know, she'll be offered the chance to move on to some livelier mission in a town or city, with a youth group and a bustling congregation of liberal, like-minded souls. And when I think of that I wonder if I'll begin my travels again then, too. But I doubt it. I belong here as much as I've ever belonged anywhere. This is where the world makes sense to me. Here I am.

My mother had no religious convictions as far as I know, but of course I lost her before reaching the age when we might have quarrelled about such things. Once though, in the hospice, very near the end, half-waking from a morphine dream, she told me she'd seen the devil, with absolute clarity, and he was a small, distant figure, walking away from her. It wasn't at all frightening, she wanted me to understand. He was walking away.

Some of the more optimistic among the Reverend Bethell's tiny flock believe in a personal God, and a personal Jesus. I prefer the thought of a personal Satan, not stinking of brimstone, more the cold scent of some stony beach, or winter fields before snow, or forestry tracks on some hillside in the rain. Where have you been? God asks him in the Book of Job. From going to and fro in the earth, he answers, and from walking up and down in it. My mother was right, I think: he always has his back to us, though we'd recognise him if he turned.

Most Sundays, in the dead hours between morning and evening services, I make my way after lunch from the cool, damp cottage that for all its smallness is much too big for me and follow the farm tracks, between fields of staring sheep, to the cliffs above the sea. I stand on the bright grass that lies like a prayer rug – wind-clipped, smooth as baize – at the very lip of the long drop down to the waves. You can watch the white backs of the gulls below, wheeling to the limed twigs of their nests, or rising and riding out on the thermals. You can see, sometimes, the black, unmoving heads of seals, solitary, or in twos and threes, pinned there among the swells and troughs. And I think of Christine, treading water over a colder, more lonely and bottomless depth, years in that hospital bed. And the night I swam out, following and losing her, turning to see the world I'd left: the orange glow of the hidden town, and somewhere within it the brief miracles of my sleeping wife and child; the fossilled cliffs crouched in their own, almost animal dark; and everything lit by the lamps of a thousand long-dead stars.